WINTER PARK LIBRARY

Ho

German:
V pronounced like F
W pronounced like V
J pronounced like Y.

The Enemy Below

By Commander Rayner:

Escort: The Battle of the Atlantic

The Enemy Below

 **The**

Enemy Below

by COMMANDER D. A. RAYNER

New York · Henry Holt and Company

87356–0117

Printed in the United States of America

Contents

The Enemy Below has been submitted to the Lords Commissioners of the British Admiralty and is published with their approval.

The Enemy Below

Author's Note

THE TALE told in this book is entirely fictional, and any similarity of names or parallel of episode is entirely coincidental.

Those who have no experience in antisubmarine warfare might contend that my tale is "too good to be true." To them I would answer that they simply do not know because, as far as I am aware, no British destroyer of the Western Approaches Escort Force ever had a prolonged single-ship action against a U-boat.

In such an action, fought with the Escort destroyers and U-boats of World War II, the odds were rather more in favor of the U-boat. She would have one or more chance of sinking her adversary by torpedo; while if she were to be forced to the surface and then should decide to carry on the action by gunfire, the target she would present would be infinitely smaller and less susceptible to damage by this weapon than that of the surface craft.

Below the water a single U-boat, pitted against a single destroyer, could turn so much more quickly that it was very difficult indeed to damage her hull by depth charges—always provided that she was handled with sufficient skill and was confident that no other surface vessel was near at hand to join her assailant. As soon as the U-boat knew for certain that two ships were present, or even thought that another ship or aircraft could be expected to join, her captain was at once forced on the defensive. The battle that I have imagined would then have run another course. For this reason I have set the scene in a very empty part of the great oceans so that both my captains are fully aware that no interference can come from a third party, and that only their own competence can decide the result.

Skill of course is the crux of the matter, and just because this is so I have postulated commanding officers of equal art and determination. Now let us see where we get to.

BOOK ONE

Radar Sparring

20.21, Zone Time, Tuesday, 7 September 1943.
Position 08° 22′ N. 30° 01′ W.

1

His majesty's destroyer *Hecate* climbed the side of each wave as it swept down upon her starboard beam, hung poised on the crest, and then slithered down the far side.

Once the motion became familiar it was no longer unpleasant. If a landsman would have thought the dizzily swaying cage to be the last word in discomfort, the two officers wedged into positions of purposeful repose in the Captain's sea cabin considered themselves to be quite at ease.

Between them on the bunk, jammed between two pillows, was a chessboard. The chessmen, that were kept in place with little pegs, had been a present to the Captain from his wife. The two officers, Captain and Doctor, played together each evening—provided always that the enemy was not expected. Of late he had been quiet on the convoy routes: now that the convoys were accompanied by the small "flat-top" escort carriers, his chances of making a successful attack were so diminished that he was almost sure of meeting a strong counterattack if he tried to force his way through the combined screen of ships and aircraft. The game of chess had therefore been an almost nightly occurrence for some months.

Leaning forward, the Captain took a white bishop with his queen. The Doctor, after due thought, lifted a knight and waved it vaguely over a square whence it would threaten the black queen.

A telephone buzzed above the Captain's head. Reaching out, he grasped it and carried it to his ear without taking his eyes from the chessboard.

"Captain's cabin," he spoke into the mouthpiece.

Both officers could hear the tinned voice of the officer of the watch: "Radar Office reports a small contact green seven-oh; range ten thousand."

"Get the plot onto it, Mackeson, and let me know its course and speed." He hung up the receiver and turned again to the game.

"It can't be a sub out here," the Doctor remarked.

"But it is!"

"How do you know, sir?"

"I'm sure of it—feel it in my bones. You know, Doc, it's a funny thing. I've often had contacts that on every evidence ought to be U-boats. I've treated them as U-boats. I've even claimed they were U-boats—either sunk or damaged. But every time I've had a contact that's made me say, 'I feel it in my bones,' it's always proved beyond a shadow of doubt to be a U-boat. More correctly, I've always known when there's been a mind matching my own at the other end of the asdic or radar beam. I feel that now. Go on. Your move, man."

The Doctor, puzzled by his Captain's passivity and desperately anxious to see his own ship in action, moved the piece he held without thinking.

The Captain's hand flicked across the board.

"Checkmate," he said.

"Damn it, sir, it's not fair. If that is a U-boat——"

"Whether it is or isn't, I can still beat you—if you let your mind wander."

"But the radar contact!"

"Was twenty degrees forward of the beam and five miles away. It was reported as a small surface echo—not an aircraft. It can't get that far away." The Captain was busily setting the chessmen back in their correct lines at each side of the board. "I wouldn't like you to whip my appendix out if you can't keep your mind on the immediate problem."

When he had finished he picked up the bridge handset.

"Mackeson, has the plot reported back yet?"

"Not yet, sir. I'll ask them." The Captain held the set to his chest. Soon it was talking again.

"Plot reports target's course approximately one-eight-oh; speed fourteen knots. Radar says the blip is quite definite, sir."

"Thank you, Mackeson. I'll be up soon. Negative zigzag." He hung up the handset and turned to his companion. "The plot will have more chance if our course is steady."

"If it is a Ube—what in the world is it doing out here?"

The Doctor had voiced the Captain's own thoughts.

"Dunno," he said as he rose and took his oilskin and sou'wester from their hook. "Let's go and ask it, shall we?"

"May I come, sir?"

"Of course, if it amuses you. I don't suppose I'll be sounding the alarm bell for some time. It's dead upwind and sea of us, and going away at fourteen knots. I doubt if we ourselves can make much more than sixteen into this weather, so it will take us some time to get there. Come on."

He went out into the dark, leaving the Doctor to shut the door behind him. Inside the cabin there had been only a dim red light. The necessity of living in red light, if his invaluable night sight was to be retained, was one of the Captain's main reasons for taking to the chessboard for relaxation. To read in red light somehow destroyed the pleasure that he could derive from a book.

The wind, warm, moist, and friendly, caressed his face as he came through the blackout flap onto the forebridge. Feeling his way to the compass platform, he acknowledged the salutes that were sensed rather than seen. Mackeson and the officer of the watch were grouped round the standard compass. The dim blue light under the swinging card was just sufficient to reveal the outline of their faces and nothing at all of their oilskin-clad figures, so that the masks, etched with deep shadows, hung bodiless in the windy night.

The bridge was alternately sheltered as the *Hecate* rolled her slim length away from the wind's onslaught, and then all at once filled with the warm tropical wind as she rolled toward the weather. Almost invisible above and behind them, the high fore-mast swept the starless night. Even the greater mass of the funnels could hardly be seen, except when sil-houetted against the fret of the ship's own wake—a disturbance of the sea that was continuously erupt-ing with livid flashes of phosphorescent light, as weird balls of blue-green fire clung tenaciously to the ship's path. Each fluorescence faded slowly into her wake but was always replaced by its fellow—newborn of her passage.

"Where is it now?" the Captain asked.

"Green oh-eight-five; range steady, sir," Mackeson answered.

"Bearing?" the Captain asked.

"Two-one-oh, sir."

"Bring her round to two-one-oh."

"Aye aye, sir."

He heard the orders given as he moved to the voice pipe that led to the plot, and felt the ship heave as her bow was brought around to head into the waves. Up she went, as if she were climbing the roof of a house. Looking aft, he could see the funnels, black against the wake. A trail of smoke from the forward one made him think that it was fortunate for the stoker on watch that it was dark. Otherwise Mackeson would have been clamoring on the engine-room telephone, and the engineer officer too would be sure to have seen it.

He bent to the voice pipe. "Forebridge—Plot."

"Plot—Forebridge."

"Captain here—what's the target doing?"

"Course about two-one-oh, sir. Speed about four-teen knots. Range has been steady."

"Who's the plotter?"

"Andrews, sir. Sick-berth attendant."

"Very well, Andrews—sure you can handle it? I don't want to go to action stations until we know more."

"Yes, sir, sure."

"Good lad."

Then, after dropping the flap cover of the voice pipe, he turned to the Doctor, who he knew was still close behind him. "Doc, after the navigator, that Andrews of yours is the best plotter in the ship."

"I'm glad he's better at that than his master is at chess."

"Does it still rankle?" The Captain laughed.

The Doctor's age was twenty-nine, and that made him, with the exception of the Captain and the elderly commissioned engineer, four years older than any other officer in the ship. Being only three years junior to the Captain, he was closer to his commanding officer in many ways than any of the others—even the excellent First Lieutenant. Consequent on their friendship a certain lack of formality existed between them.

"Sure, it rankles like hell."

The Captain crossed to the compass platform in the center of the bridge, whence a voice pipe led direct to the Radar Office.

"Forebridge—Radar."

"Radar—Forebridge."

"Who's on the set?"

"Petty Officer Lewis, sir."

The Captain wondered how Lewis had got word that something was happening. He should not have been on watch until action stations had been sounded, for he was not normally a watchkeeper. His duties were to keep the set functioning properly and to man it only in action. Already the Captain guessed that the whole ship knew that they had a suspicious radar contact. The ship, where men were keyed to intense awareness of a cruel and able enemy forever on the lookout for them, was a most efficient sounding board. He was glad Lewis was there. Not because he was a good petty officer—he was not. Untidy himself, and incapable of maintaining discipline, he owed his promotion entirely to his ability to maintain and work his set—and in this he had few equals.

"What's it look like, Lewis?" the Captain asked.

"Small, sharp blip, sir. Just about right for a U-boat, sir."

"Thank you. I'm going to increase speed now. Press the bell if you find that the extra vibration is spoiling your reception on the set." He raised his face from the pipe. "Mr. Mackeson, increase to two hundred revolutions."

"Aye aye, sir."

The Captain went to rejoin the Doctor who, without an oilskin to protect him, had pressed himself up against the front of the bridge and was sheltering behind the thick plate-glass screens. Now that her head was to the sea, the screens were slashed with runnels of spray; and only the two fast-revolving discs of the Kent Clearview Screens gave them an easy view ahead.

The engine-room ratings answered the Captain's call, and as he came up beside the Doctor he felt the deck beneath his feet begin to throb with ever faster pulsations. The *Hecate* heaved her body half out of the water—a body in whose forepart were crowded over a hundred and forty human beings. Those off watch swung in their hammocks that hung, like monstrous cocoons, from the deckhead and swayed largely sideways and slightly back and forth in fantastic unison as the ship moved. The hammocks were indistinguishable in their similarity—only the names stamped on their bottoms were different. It was curious that in the identical cocoons the individuals were so unlike.

Now the ship was plunging downward with the powerful drive of her propellers forcing her into the next sea. A wall of water, pale gray in the blackness, flooded over her bow. She shuddered, paused as a horse will do to gather its haunches beneath it, and then shot skyward once more; and the wave top, running aft along her length, burst against the forward screen. Clouds of water, salt-tasting and very wet, were flung over the bridge. The sea cascaded in arched bands of foam from the rising bows. There was a moment when she was swept only by the wind—when only the drops of glistening water were wind-whipped away. Then she was going down again, down into the next sea's flank—cutting it, shivering with the strain.

"It's too much," the Captain shouted to the Doctor. "I'll have to ease her down." And to the officer of the watch, whose water-glistening oilskins caught the wild light from the phosphorescent waves: "Ease her down to one-five-oh, Mr. Mackeson."

The shuddering ceased as the speed was reduced. The clicking of the pitometer log fell in sympathetic rallentando. The bell from the Radar Office buzzed angrily.

"Forebridge," the Captain called.

"Fair shook the set up that last one, sir."

"All right, Lewis. I've eased her down—I won't increase again until the sea moderates. Still holding contact?"

"Yes, sir. Target's still there. Dead ahead now, sir, range nine thousand."

"Thank you, Lewis." Back to the Doctor: "I'm dead sure it's a U-boat. Don't ask me what it's doing —but I'm sure it is one. It's too small to be anything but that, or a fishing boat; and there are no fishing boats in this deserted piece of ocean, and none that can steam at fourteen knots into this sea. I do believe it's going to give me just what I've always wanted. A single-ship duel between a U-boat and a destroyer without any chance of anyone interfering."

"What odds would you lay?"

"So near 'evens' that I'd really have to know the other captain, Doc. As far as the ships are concerned, I'd just put my money on the U-boat."

"But you reckon you'll win?"

"Of course. Both of us will think that. The Hun and I. We've got to think like that—otherwise we'd crack. If he's the man I hope he is, we'll have a wonderful hunt."

"In this weather?"

"The sea will have gone down before dawn. This little gale is very local. These subtropical areas are full of them. The one we are enjoying at the moment is a rather large one of its kind."

"Captain, sir." A new figure had joined them.

"Hullo, Number One, have we got you out of your bunk?"

21

"Just turning in, sir, when you altered course. Thought I'd come up to see if you wanted me. I'd hardly started along the iron deck when you increased speed, and I had to dodge back mighty quick."

"We've got a possible radar contact on a U-boat. We're chasing dead up his tail, and he's four and a half miles ahead. I don't think I'll get any closer until the weather moderates. It will anyway by dawn, and we're running out of it at fourteen knots. Nine o'clock now; nine hours until dawn at fourteen knots. A hundred and twenty-six miles to the southwest when dawn comes—if he doesn't spot us before."

"He's almost certain to do that. He's got radar too."

"But no radar mattress aft. He's got to swing his ship if he wants to get a bearing on anything that's right behind him. If we keep station on him—always there—always in station, it's my bet his radar operator will think it's a ghost echo. We've had them ourselves so often. If we were to go playing about—closing up on him, or drawing off to one side, then he'd know us for what we are. Am I right?"

"Sounds very foxy to me, sir. But I see your point. If we scare him and put him down in this sea, our asdic will be pretty useless, and he'll probably give us the slip."

"Exactly, Number One." And to the officer of the watch: "Mr. Mackeson, I want to keep station exactly ten thousand yards astern of the target until four o'clock tomorrow morning."

"Take station ten thousand yards astern of target, sir," Mackeson repeated.

"Better get your head down, Number One." The Captain addressed his First Lieutenant.

Willis, the yeoman, was hovering around the three officers, his signal pad in his hand. He coughed to announce his presence.

"Yeoman," the Captain said, "are you itching to make a signal? I don't think it's necessary until we know for sure. We can signal then."

"We'll be a long way off our proper course by then, sir," the First Lieutenant reminded him.

"Almost one hundred and thirty miles," the Captain agreed. "But we've got a hell of a fast ship. If we're wrong and our friend turns out to be a Brazilian fishing boat that's gone gaga, we can slip back easily without anyone being the wiser. No, Yeoman, sorry to disappoint you. No signal yet."

"Good night, sir," the First Lieutenant said.

" 'Night, Number One."

The Doctor spoke softly at the Captain's elbow when the other two had gone: "There could be another reason for not making a signal."

"Meaning?"

"Less chance of interference."

"God blast your impudence. If you were an executive officer I'd put you under close arrest." There was genuine friendship and amusement in the Captain's voice.

"I'm your medical adviser. For your professional secrets my lips are sealed."

"Your doom's sealed as a chess player."

"Good night, sir."

"Good night, doc."

"Good luck."

He was alone in the wind. The ship rode easily now that her speed was still further reduced. She crept after her quarry—the heart of her purring like a great cat, and the snaking tail of her wake laid flat to the waves over which she had stalked.

Taking each decision separately, the Captain turned over the events of the last hour. As he did so the continuous note of the asdic impinged on his conscious mind.

"Mr. Mackeson. Tell the asdic hut to cease transmissions and to keep a listening watch only." The pings of the asdic under good conditions could be heard at great distances and might well bolt this particular fox.

Silence again on the windswept bridge, and time once more to think and query his actions. He had been frankly troubled by the Doctor's remark, even though it may have been a lighthearted one. Was it true that he had refrained from sending a signal because he wanted so badly to fight his individual battle? His mind, trained to react to emergencies, sometimes worked so fast that it was difficult to tell, even to himself, where instinct ended and thought began. To challenge single-handed such a deadly foe was to risk needlessly his ship and the lives of some, if not all, of his men. Yet his instinct had been all against breaking wireless silence.

The unusual position must be considered in some detail.

His target, if it were indeed a U-boat, was obviously going somewhere with a very definite object. Even allowing that a U-boat represented too much of her nation's energy to be permitted to cruise aimlessly far from the convoy routes, the speed of this particular boat suggested considerable urgency. At fourteen knots, and steaming into that sea, conditions aboard would be extremely unpleasant and would greatly reduce the normal efficiency of her crew. Indeed, her own haste might well have reduced the effectiveness of her detecting equipment, so that he had been able to fall in astern of her without being observed.

What could she be up to? To land agents on the coast of Brazil? Her present course suggested a destination farther down the coast of the South American continent. To refuel in the neutral Argentine? Her speed suggested a certain prodigality with fuel, but it was a possibility. He wished he knew to what rendezvous she hurried.

For a moment his mind digressed to ponder on his horror of foreign words in the English language, however appropriate they might be.

Rendezvous? Then he understood! The U-boat was steaming to meet a supply ship in this deserted part of the ocean, or an armed merchant raider, or—his mind boggled at the thought—even a German pocket battleship. In his imagination he saw himself having to break off an engagement with a U-boat to take over the duties of a cruiser: the duties of detecting and shadowing, while superior forces were collected in order that the enemy might with certainty be destroyed.

If this hypothesis were in any way correct, it was even more important not to flush the bird too soon. A signal would stand a good chance of being monitored by the efficient German radio service. With stations on the long coastline from the North Cape to Dakar, they would obtain a reliable idea of his position and would warn the U-boat and whatever it was going to meet. Judgment must be very nice. He must make a signal as soon as the submarine dived, and hope to hold it down so that it could not surface to receive a warning. He must make his signal very short and hope to avoid the German monitors. It took time, he knew, to line up the direction-finding sets onto a signal. He must explain the position to Johnson, the petty officer telegraphist, and try to get him to pass the signal in something less than five minutes. Johnson would, of course, use the emergency prefix which would insure his signal receiving priority.

Brains in the Admiralty would think faster and know more of the background than he did. But the U-boat must first be sighted. A report based on a suspicious but unclassified radar echo might cause error and uncertainty in London. What should he say? *"U-boat sighted on surface, seen to submerge,"* and then give the geographical position? The Admiralty could do the rest of the thinking . . . or could they? What did he know that he would not be telling them? The steady course! He must tell them that, if they were to give proper weight to the occurrence. He'd alter the signal to read: *"Have tracked U-boat by radar for 130 miles, submerged after identification,"* then the position. Mentally he crossed out the words *"after identification"* and substituted *"at dawn."* It would be equally strong and helped to explain his tracking a wily enemy for so long.

He was so pleased with the result of his thinking that he almost felt like waking up the Doctor just to tell him.

"Mr. Mackeson, how's the target?"

"Two-one-oh; ten thousand, sir."

"Good. Keep it so."

He crossed to the telephone to the Radar Office and picked up the handset. "Lewis," he said when he heard the petty officer's voice answering. "Are you getting tired?"

"No, sir. I'm all right. I can carry on until dawn if you wish."

"I'd feel happier if you were about. We shan't need you once the light comes. I don't expect you to stay on the set all the time. Just keep handy."

"Aye aye, sir."

Lewis, the Captain thought, was a great asset. Bad petty officer he might be, but his set was mother, father, wife, and child to him. He turned to Mackeson.

"Eleven-thirty now. I'm going down to my sea cabin. I'll be up at once if you want me. I'll just lie down and rest. I want to be fresh when the dawn comes. Call me at once if you're in any doubt. The navigator's got the middle watch, and Number One the morning. I'm to be called at four-thirty, and leave a message for the First Lieutenant to see there's a dam' great cup of 'kai' waiting for me."

"Will you have a cup now, sir?"

"Yes, if there's any being brewed. Tell the bosun's mate to bring a cup to my cabin. Good night, Mackeson."

"Good night, sir."

It was good to get out of his clumsy oilskins and stretch out on his bunk. The thick hot cup of kai was as warming to the stomach as it was satisfying to the mind. The drink was as much a meal as liquid refreshment. On the bridge the chocolate would have solidified in a rim around the cup, but here in the warm cabin it tasted like a hot chocolate mousse. He licked his lips appreciatively. The Americans, he had heard, drank coffee on the bridge at sea. He thanked heaven he was in the British Navy.

The ship rose and fell sedately. The regular pitching was accompanied by only the very slightest roll. As her bow was borne upward, he felt that his body, stretched on the bunk, was pressed cosily down upon the mattress. When the long, lean bow plunged downward, his body pressed less heavily upon its resting place. It was a sensation that never failed to please him.

He heard the clattering of feet as the watch was changed at midnight. After a decent interval he raised the handset from the bridge telephone beside his head.

"Forebridge, sir." The voice rolled the r's with Scottish persistence. "For-r-bridge, sorr."

"Is everything under control, Pilot?"

"Yes, sir."

"Good. I'm here if you want me."

"Thank you, sir."

He replaced the set. He ought to sleep, he knew, but sleep had never seemed farther away than it did at the moment. His excitement was too great. Tomorrow he would be trying to kill a violent enemy; and just as certainly the U-boat captain would be trying to kill him. Sleep to refresh the mind was greatly to be desired, if only because the battle would in great measure be fought with the mind and will of the opposing captains—but sleep eluded him. Before long he became resigned to the inevitability of a watch night. If he could only obtain bodily rest instead of the mental oblivion he sought, he could at least turn the waiting hours to good account by devoting them to thought—and this might well give him an initial advantage over his adversary.

If he had guessed correctly, some instrument aboard the U-boat was not functioning. Something had gone wrong with her delicate susceptibilities, and he was confident that her Kapitan was sleeping calmly, quite oblivious of the fact that an enemy was sitting on his tail.

Sooner or later the U-boat's Kapitan would discover the unwelcome fact. The conditions inside the boat at that moment leapt to the imagination and brought a smile to his lips. There would be anger, disorder, and bitter recriminations, and none of these emotions would help the efficiency of the underwater machine. They were all a poor prelude to a battle, where wits and personal skill would count for so much. In turn these would be followed by righteous indignation on one part and by sulkiness on the other—a canker of doubt on either side. It was not to be expected, however, that these disagreements would for long impair the efficiency of the very efficient German U-boat service. Soon, or very soon, depending on his personal qualities, the Kapitan would have his boat working smoothly again. He'd begin to weigh the situation, either speedily and by instinct or more slowly and with thorough precision. Either course could be right, depending on the man's nature.

He thought that the German would want to see what was happening, and what were the odds against him. Taken by surprise, he'd probably only have secondhand information about his assailant. He'd almost certainly risk a peep through his periscope; and on what he then saw he would make up his mind whether to risk firing torpedoes or not. If he could be sure that only one ship was following him, he'd almost certainly attempt to torpedo her—because to do so would at once remove all his worries. Bow or stern tubes? It made a difference between two or four torpedoes; but in the relative positions of the ships, to turn the U-boat would waste too much time. He'd fire both stern tubes. Assuming that the U-boat would dive four miles away from the destroyer, the *Hecate* would cover the distance in fifteen minutes. She could hardly be driven faster up sea, or the water noise would be so great that it would interfere with the reception of her delicate asdic machine. This would allow a resourceful man plenty of time to plan and execute a torpedo attack. A torpedo would cover the narrowing distance in about two minutes, but it would take five minutes to work out the settings, put them on the torpedoes, and fire them.

Mentally the Captain did his sum. Five minutes for the Kapitan to regain control of his boat after the crash dive. Five minutes to set and fire the torpedoes. A large alteration of course ten minutes after the submarine dived should take him clear of his enemy's riposte. But would it? A ship did not answer immediately. She took time to turn, and her momentum would keep her moving in the old direction even though her bow was turning to the new course. It would be better to give the order for the step aside at eight minutes after diving. Then, by calculation, there would be one desperate minute when the Kapitan, his torpedoes running, would see his adversary turn and know that his lunge would pass harmlessly over his enemy's shoulder. The Captain hoped this would be the case—it would be a great disappointment to the German.

The more he thought of it, the more important it seemed to the Captain that he should draw his enemy's fangs as soon as he could. He hoped to give the German no peace in which to reload once he was within asdic range, and certainly no time in which to fire his bow tubes. The real danger from torpedoes existed only in the time that it would take the *Hecate* to close in from four miles to one mile. Once he was inside that distance, and provided he could hold contact with the enemy, it would be almost impracticable for the U-boat to attempt to torpedo him. Even if he had no depth charges with which to harry or burst open his opponent, the U-boat could not remain submerged indefinitely. She must surface at the end of twenty-four hours—so the textbooks said—to recharge the batteries and replenish the air, both for human breathing and for the air bottles that worked her ballast tanks.

He looked at his watch. It was already past two o'clock. He heard the clatter of steps down the ladder outside his door. Guessing their purport, he raised the bridge telephone from its hook.

"Captain, sir?" the query came at once. It would take a clever man to catch the navigator napping.

"How's the kai boat, Pilot?"

"Bosun's mate's just gone to brew some, sir."

"I'll have a cup. How's our friend the enemy?"

"Aye aye, sir. Oh, the enemy's still doing a steady fourteen knots. Very easy fellow to keep station on.

Five revolutions up or down every quarter of an hour, that's all the alterations I've had to make since I came on, and his course is still two-one-oh, sir."

"How's the weather? It feels as if it's easing."

"Easing quite a bit now, sir. I can see a star or two."

"Is the wind veering at all?"

"No, sir. Steady as rock. It's just dying away, or we're running out of it."

"Probably both, Pilot. Keep up the good work." The Captain replaced the handset.

The bosun's mate brought him the cocoa. Sipping it appreciatively, he went once more carefully over his previous thoughts. There seemed little to alter in the picture his imagination had drawn, and only one point that worried him. Would a U-boat fire torpedoes at a destroyer approaching dead toward him? It seemed a terribly small target at which to aim. But suppose he were deliberately to tempt the German by offering him an easier shot—would that be more likely to draw the enemy's sting? If he altered course as soon as the U-boat dived by thirty degrees to starboard, the maneuver, even if the Kapitan observed it, would be readily understood as a desire on the part of the British ship to get away from that attack which was always so difficult—the one where the quarry was running straight away from the attacker. Then eight minutes later he would alter the *Hecate's* course sixty degrees to port.

This certainly seemed to be the solution. Throw away the "Knight of speed" in order to gain the "Queen of drawn claws." It was a game of chess played with the ocean for board, ships for pieces, and men's lives for stakes.

2

U-BOAT *121* hurried over the sea. Driving her into the waves regardless of the devastating motion, the powerful diesels shook her strong hull with vibration, and their clatter pervaded the whole boat. As her bow rocketed skyward men's innards would be left behind. As the lean ship breasted the wave's crest, she would corkscrew wildly before plunging downward, and once again stomachs would be in suspension. It was a motion that was sufficient to nauseate the toughest, and conditions aboard were indescribably vile.

Korvettenkapitan Peter von Stolberg had a stomach that was never proof against such violent motion. Consequently, after refusing his supper, he had turned into his bunk, where, with pills, he had tried to calm the queasiness within him. Only necessity, the urgent necessity, of getting to a given position on the deserted ocean by a given time had caused him to make this high-speed dash on the surface. It had to be done regardless of the discomfort to the crew and the possibility of damage to his ship, because the Grand Admiral had said that he must be there on time. The Kapitan could see the shrewd, dynamic face of his superior as he closed his eyes to shut out the misery of his and his men's condition.

"You will be in position by noon, local time, on the ninth of September, Herr Kapitan—and nothing must stop you. Nothing!" The little man had slammed his fist on the polished top of the great desk behind which he sat. His eyes, of an unnaturally pale blue with irises completely surrounded by the whites, appeared like those of a bullfrog—about to pop out of his head. "Raider M has succeeded in capturing a complete set of the Allied ciphers that the enemy will bring into force on the first of October. It is true she is herself coming home, with a pleasant load of prisoners, after sinking over a hundred thousand tons of enemy shipping—but that is not certain enough for me. You understand? We must insure against the risk of her nonarrival. She has been instructed to photograph the ciphers and transfer the films to you, for delivery to me here. You are to proceed direct to this position and, unless you yourself are directly attacked, you are not to engage the enemy—however tempting the target may be."

A few days later *U-121* had sailed from Brest, apparently with plenty of time to make the rendezvous. But the first few days had not been entirely happy. A patrolling Liberator had spotted them on the second night out, and they had suddenly found themselves under the bright, artificial moon of a parachute flare. A moment later the sea around them had erupted as the stick of depth charges burst. Worse was to follow.

A British escort group of sloops had hunted his boat relentlessly for three days before he had finally been able to shake them off. Thus they had been forced to make almost the whole of the first eight hundred miles submerged—surfacing only at irregular intervals and for just enough time to recharge their batteries. The continual air reconnaissance of the British Coastal Command was no longer a joke.

When at length the Kapitan had his boat clear of the aircraft, he had run into persistent bad weather; and the margin of seven days which he had thought he had in hand when he left Brest had gradually been whittled down to no more than a bare eighteen hours to spare. For that reason, and that alone, he was driving his ship and his men unmercifully. At the same time he was extremely angry with his own frailty. He disliked the motion and he hated the stench of sickness that pervaded the boat. But the pill he had taken was working now. He felt drowsy. Soon he was asleep, rolling slightly from side to side. The expression of disgust still curled his lips, for he was a fastidious man.

Leutnant-zur-See Erich Kunz had the first watch. He was concerned only with keeping himself as dry as possible, and that was a difficult enough job. Crash would go the long bow into the steep head sea, flinging up the spray to whip over the exposed conning tower. Then the wave, roaring aft along the deck, would break in fury against the four-inch gun, sending even heavier water pouring over the men who crouched in their inadequate shelter. There were three men whose duty kept them outside: Kunz, the officer of the watch, Karl Schott the signalman, and a seaman for lookout. It was, thought Kunz, a useless duty for all three, for in no direction could their water-washed eyes see a thing. But he dared not say so to his commanding officer.

A head and shoulders appeared above the conning-tower hatch. "Radar operator says it's time to swing her, sir."

"Very well," Kunz acknowledged the information. Through the voice pipe he ordered the alteration of course that would enable one of the quarter radar mattresses to cover the arc where the stern had been. Unlike a surface ship, whose radar aerial turned continually, the U-boats had "send and receive" radar mattresses that were fixed around the conning tower, each covering a certain arc. But because of the positioning of the antiaircraft gun there was no mattress that covered the arc that lay ten degrees on either side of the stern. Consequently when on passage the routine practice was to swing the boat twenty degrees to one side once every hour to make sure that nothing was astern—and when this was ascertained to turn back once more to their course.

A moment or two later the head and shoulders reappeared.

"Anything to report?" Kunz asked.

"The ground returns from the sea are so bad that the screen's cluttered up with false echoes, Herr Leutnant."

"Who is the operator?"

"Bauer."

Kunz nodded. "Very well." Willi Bauer was the signalman responsible for looking after the radar set. His report should be reliable.

"Bauer said that there seems to be a ghost echo eleven thousand meters astern—very indefinite."

"Anything would be in this weather. There're no surface ships here, and if there are—we can't attack them."

"Shall I report to the Kapitan?"

"No—no. He will be angry if he is disturbed."

"Zum Befehl, Herr Leutnant." *(as you order)*

"Tell Bauer to see if it's still there in an hour's time."

The head and shoulders disappeared. "Bring her back on course," Kunz said into the voice pipe, and he settled down to another hour of misery.

An hour later the ghost was still there.

"That proves it's something in the set—that machine is haunted with ghosts. Tell the hydrophone operator to see if he can hear any asdic transmissions, and report to me."

"Zum Befehl, Herr Leutnant."

Five minutes later the messenger was back again. "No transmissions audible, sir."

"Thank you." Kunz, satisfied that the radar had chosen this occasion to trot out one of the innumerable ghost echoes of which it was capable, continued to do his utmost to keep himself dry.

And so it had gone on. From hour to hour and from watch to watch. The longer that the echo stayed just where it was, the more likely it was to be a "ghost." For who had ever heard of an escort that, obtaining a radar contact, had not rushed at it full tilt?

Kunz had been relieved at midnight by Oberleutnant Otto von Holem. There was no love lost between these two. Kunz considered von Holem a useless sprig of the nobility, and von Holem thought that Kunz was beneath contempt. The exchange had been as short as the necessity of duty permitted. At the last moment

37

Kunz had paused halfway down the hatch. "Oberleutnant, there is a ghost echo on the radar eleven thousand meters astern. I forgot to tell you."

"You have reported it to the Kapitan?"

"No. It was reported as a ghost and has been there for three hours. It can be nothing else."

Von Holem was about to suggest with some acerbity that the Kapitan should have been told when Kunz added from one rung farther down the hatch: "I thought you'd like the pleasure of stirring up a hornets' nest."

"Verfluchter Kerl," von Holem murmured and turned to duck as a solid sheet of water flung itself over the conning tower.

Four hours later von Holem was relieved by the Executive Officer, Oberleutnant Heini Schwachofer.

"The weather improves."

"It's not quite so wet now."

The two officers stood side by side looking over the long bow as it creamed into a wave. But the wind was gone, and only a spatter of spray fell into the conning tower.

"Anything to report?"

"Nothing. A ghost echo turned up in Kunz's watch. Dead astern eleven thousand. I nearly reported it to the Kapitan, but it's so regularly there that I'm sure it is a ghost. It's been there now for eight hours."

"I agree. It can't be the enemy. He's not the patient sort. Anyway there are no escorts in this part of the world. Sleep well, Otto."

Von Holem lowered himself down the hatch.

The watch dragged on. A pale sheen flitted on the advancing face of the waves. The hull appeared darker

and the phosphorescence paler—the dawn. Schwachofer stirred, easing cramped limbs.

"Signalman, coffee."

The man disappeared.

The cold light grew in intensity. The horizon of
exact sight expanded, fifty meters—two hundred meters.

The signalman thrust a cup of steaming coffee into
his hand.

"Ah!" The Executive Officer put salt-caked lips to
the hot rim. The scent of coffee filled his nostrils.
"Ah!" he said again with satisfaction.

The dawn of a new day crept over the ocean. It
was lighter to the east. He glanced at his watch—
twenty minutes past six—and turned again to look
over the bow. The wave motion fascinated him as the
seas creamed along the U-boat's circular hull and
sucked at the long casing that ran up to the high bow.

Putting the binoculars to his eyes, he began a routine sweep. Jagged wave tops ahead, long valleys on the
beam, the smooth backs of retreating waves astern
and— (To the devil —a curse)

"Zum Teufel!" He lowered his glasses, wiped them
hurriedly, and looked again. Then he stretched out his
hand and pressed the alarm for emergency diving stations.

The strident roar of the klaxon, that had not been
heard for the last fortnight, filled the boat. In a moment the narrow central alleyway was full of men hurrying to their stations. They hauled themselves from
their bunks, struggled into jackets, fastened trouser
belts, grumbling and cursing. U-boat *121* had been
caught with her pants down.

39

3

SUBMARINE DIVING, sir."

The cry was taken up by many voices.

"Commence asdic sweep: steer two-four-oh: note the time, Pilot. Yeoman, get a position from the navigator and get that signal off right away, Johnson is expecting it. Number One, sound off action stations and let me know as soon as the seven minutes are up." The Captain's orders came crisply and with certainty.

The telephone from the radar cabinet buzzed. The Captain raised the handset. "Forebridge."

"Echo's faded, sir." Lewis' voice sounded tired.

"Thank you, Lewis. We've seen the U-boat submerge—and thank you for your work. It's been a dam' fine effort."

"Thank you, sir."

"Go and get your head down, man. I'll send for you if I need you."

"Aye aye, sir."

The Captain replaced the handset. While he had been talking he had been conscious of many feet clattering up ladders; the clang of iron as some hatches were closed and clipped, and other hatches, up which the ammunition would be sent to the guns, were flung open. Now the apparent chaos had subsided to the quiet efficiency of a prepared ship. The *Hecate* had drawn her sword, and the naked blade was bright in her hand.

From many places came the reports.

"Coxswain at the wheel, sir."

"B Gun cleared away, sir."

"Depth-charge crews correct, sir."

"Asdic hut closed up, sir."

"Plot closed up, sir."

"X Gun cleared away, sir."

"Third boiler connected, sir."

It was, the Captain thought, an evolution that never ceased to thrill—action stations sounded in the presence of the enemy. The incredibly intricate ship coming under the control of one brain. Not that the one brain functioned alone: it planned the action but left the carrying out to trusted officers. Mentally he reviewed them. There wasn't one who could not be relied upon to do his job.

The First Lieutenant touched his arm.

"Seven minutes, sir."

"In one minute alter course to port to one-eight-oh. Use thirty degrees of wheel. If she does not turn fast enough I'll stop the port engine. I want her on the new course in two minutes."

"Aye aye, sir."

The Captain moved apart from the other officers clustered on the bridge. He felt an immediate desire to be alone—for he looked fear in the face and wanted to meet this new adversary alone. It was not so much the personal fear of death but the fear that his professional judgment might prove to be at fault. Somewhere on the port bow and hidden by the waves he was sure that there was a lethal enemy preparing to strike at him, and through him at the ship he commanded and at the men who trusted him. For the first time in the whole war he had had the time to seriously plan a meeting with the enemy. Previous engagements had been fought on snap decisions and intuitive actions. Parry had followed riposte into lunge with such speed that serious thought had been impossible. This carefully calculated action was foreign both to his nature and to his experience.

The sun was breaking the horizon's rim. Pale gold light dispersed the last of the dawn's shadow.

"Port thirty, steer one-eight-oh." He heard the First Lieutenant's voice giving the incisive order, and he moved toward the standard compass. The *Hecate* began to heel, to lean over to starboard as her rudder bit into the water. Looking astern, the slick, satin smooth, was seen to be already growing from her port quarter.

The telephone from the asdic cabinet broke the silence. The Captain's arm shot out, and then remembering that he of all people must remain calm, he slowly raised the handset to his face. "Forebridge."

The asdic officer's excited voice came to him: "Strong hydrophone effect on port bow."

"Bearing?" the Captain snapped.

"Difficult to say, sir. It covers quite a large arc. I'd say red three-oh to right ahead."

The Captain looked at his First Lieutenant. "How's her head?"

"Passing two-one-oh, sir."

Captain to asdic cabinet: "Bearing now?"

Asdic cabinet to Captain: "Seems to be crossing the bow, sir. Approximate center bearing red oh-five to green one-oh. Getting much louder, sir."

Captain to First Lieutenant: "How's her head?"

"Passing one-nine-eight, sir."

Captain down voice pipe to the wheelhouse: "Stop port."

The voice pipe answered: "Port engine stopped, sir."

Captain to First Lieutenant: "Half ahead port engine as soon as you're round to one-eight-five."

"Aye aye, sir."

Captain to asdic cabinet: "Bearing now?"

"Green oh-five to green six-oh."

By the record of their instruments the torpedoes had crossed their bows and were speeding into the barren wastes of the sea, where they would sink to the bottom and lie on the ooze, to the astonishment of the deep-sea fish. But one could never be quite certain unless one's eyes could confirm the tale told by the clever electrical machines.

"Captain, sir! Captain, sir!" The bridge lookout on the starboard searchlight platform was pointing desperately toward the starboard beam.

Hurrying across the bridge, the Captain leaned over the starboard side to follow the lookout's finger. There, lying across the now blue and sparkling water, were two long white shafts that undulated as the waves crossed their path.

He came back to the compass platform. "Two torpedoes passed down our starboard side—half a cable clear." He felt good. He felt grand. He went to the voice pipe that led to the plot. "Pilot, give me a course to a position two-one-oh degrees three miles from where she dived."

A moment's wait and then from the pipe the Scot's accent: "Two-oh-eight, sir."

"Thank you." The Captain turned to the First Lieutenant, who had just ordered the port engine ahead again. "Bring her back to two-oh-eight. We've drawn his fangs."

"Starboard thirty, steer two-oh-eight." The order was passed, and then: "Worked a treat, sir." His First Lieutenant's smiling face was raised to his, the blue eyes laughing in the tanned face. "I bet the Herr Kapitan is hopping mad."

"I hope so too. It may get him rattled—but I doubt it. He's the fighting type or he'd never have sent those kippers after us. He'll give us a run for our money."

Willis, the yeoman, approached him.

"Yes, Yeoman?"

"Message passed, sir. Johnson told me to tell you 'four minutes ten seconds dead,' sir."

"Thank you, Yeoman. Pass the word to Johnson that I'm very pleased indeed with the time. It's dam' good."

The *Hecate* was heeling now to port as she turned back to starboard after her enemy. Astern, her wake showed clear—a gigantic S, the turns almost half a mile in diameter. Leaning against the voice pipe to the wheelhouse, the Captain could hear snatches of conversation not meant for his ears.

"What I wants to know is how the Old Man knew the bastard was going to try to kipper us."

" 'Cos he's got a head on, hasn't he—same as you. The difference is that he uses his. That's what he draws his pay for."

Laughing, the Captain flicked over the cover of the voice pipe, cutting off further chance of eavesdropping.

The bell from the asdic buzzed.

"Forebridge," the Captain said.

"Submarine echo bearing two-oh-eight, sir. Going away, extreme range."

"Nice job, Hopkins. Keep the plot informed." And to the plot: "Asdic has a target bearing two-oh-eight degrees, probably submarine. Extreme range. Plot the target."

"Aye aye, sir. Plot the target."

4

OBERLEUTNANT SCHWACHOFER, after he had clipped down the heavy lower conning-tower hatch, jumped the last four rungs to the deck and steadied himself by holding onto the ladder.

Already the boat's bow was sinking and the deck inclined downward. The clatter of the diesels had gone, and in its place was the soft purr of the big electric motors. The Kapitan came from the doorway that led to the wardroom and thence to the engine and motor rooms. He was unshaven, had pouches under his eyes, and did not look well. His hurriedly donned coat was unfastened and the trousers, in which he had slept, were crumpled.

"What is it?" He spoke in a voice that was louder than necessary, causing his Executive Officer to fear needlessly for his Kapitan's nerve.

"A British destroyer, Herr Kapitan."

"Nonsense! Did you sight her?"

"Indeed I did. Between four and five miles astern."

"To the eastward of us up sun. It is possible that she has not sighted us."

"I fear, Herr Kapitan"—Schwachofer was going cautiously in spite of the obvious need to tell his senior everything that he knew—"that she has been tailing us since just after eight o'clock last night. We—that is first Kunz, and then the rest of us—thought that it was a ghost echo."

"Impossible." The veins were standing out in the Kapitan's neck. "Impossible!" The blood was coursing into his face. The Executive Officer had never seen such fury. "Impossible!" Schwachofer drew back as if he feared his Kapitan would strike him.

The Kapitan shivered as, with a great effort, he fought for control and succeeded in achieving the mastery of his temper. But when he spoke the tone of his voice was unrecognizable for the friendly manner.

"Blöde Kerls. (stupid fellows) All of you. Almost ten hours. One hundred and forty miles you have brought the enemy. You know how important is our mission, and you lead him to our rendezvous. Is this how *U-121* obeys the orders of the Grand Admiral?"

"I'm sorry, Herr Kapitan."

"Mistakes cannot be rectified in war. Please God the Britisher makes a mistake. Four and a half miles. Bring the boat to ten meters at once. At once, you understand. I would use the periscope."

Both officers glanced at the depth gauge that already showed sixty meters. The Kapitan's standing order was that, on the sounding of the crash-dive signal, the boat should be taken down to eighty meters.

The Executive Officer issued sharp orders. The bow whose dip had been growing less, now became level. The hiss of high pressure air stowed in the big bottles under the deck could be heard expelling the water from the ballast tanks. The needle of the depth gauge stopped, hovered, and began to retrace its steps— slowly at first, and then more quickly.

The Kapitan buttoned up his coat as he watched the gauge. One hand stroked his chin. He wished he could have been given time to shave. He did not like the men to see their Kapitan looking disheveled.

Twenty meters. The needle crept more slowly now.

"Course two-one-oh. Four knots. Periscope depth, Herr Oberleutnant—and be prepared to dive deep."

The hiss of the hydraulic rods, that brought the big attack periscope from its well, sounded through the control room. The eyepiece with its handles appeared above the deck. Bending, the Kapitan seized them. His back unbent as the periscope continued to rise. His eyes were fixed in the rubber eyeshield.

"Ten meters," Schwachofer spoke crisply. Now that his Kapitan was taking the offensive, his own morale was returning. They'd sink the destroyer and then, in the rejoicing, they'd all be forgiven. He could even imagine that an unscrupulous Kapitan might claim to have lured the intruder along until daylight so that he could torpedo it. He wondered just how scrupulous von Stolberg was. A strong disciplinarian, a good fellow, but a real Junker. Schwachofer was a sailor, born and bred in the Baltic timber trade; he would not altogether trust a "von."

At the Kapitan's touch the periscope rose still higher until he was standing upright. Schwachofer watched von Stolberg's feet move flatly, gripping the deck that, now that they were at periscope depth, was feeling again the effect of the surface waves.

The Kapitan spoke: "She is not astern." A pause

—then: "Ach—I have her now, bearing green one-six-oh. A Western Approaches destroyer. She has the white and light green camouflage. Converted for escort work. One of the forward, one of the after guns, and the torpedo tubes have been taken out of her so that she may carry more depth charges."

"She was astern," Schwachofer volunteered.

"Then she makes her big mistake." The Kapitan's voice was gleeful. "Her Captain is a clever man. He thinks to work out on my beam before he comes in to attack. An attack up my stern is so difficult for him. He will lose contact so long before he must fire his depth charges that I shall avoid them. So he plans to attack from my beam. But, Schwachofer, I shall sink him. Kunz, start the attack table."

"Jawohl, Herr Kapitan." Kunz, its attendant officer, started the complicated electrical device that, when fed with the enemy's course, speed, and range, would provide the angle of deflection that, when set on the sight in the periscope, would enable the torpedoes to be aimed just the right amount ahead of the target in order that target and torpedoes should arrive at the same place and at the same time. The Kapitan himself, knowing the length of the enemy, would decide on the amount of spread between one torpedo and the next.

"Müller," the Kapitan called the torpedo petty officer. "Prepare numbers five and six tubes; set torpedoes to run at three meters at forty knots."

"Jawohl, Herr Kapitan." The man disappeared aft.

"Kunz. Enemy's bearing green one-five-five, course two-four-oh. Speed one-five knots. Range eight thousand five hundred."

The hush of excitement settled on every man in the

boat. Their heartbeats were caught up in the steady purr of the engines.

The periscope hissed as the Kapitan lowered it.

"Well?" he said, turning to Kunz.

"Deflection two-five degrees left, Herr Kapitan."

"Zum Befehl." The Kapitan bent to the periscope handles and raised them slowly. "Stand by numbers five and six tubes."

"Müller reports numbers five and six ready, Herr Kapitan."

"Gut." (good)

The periscope was nearly up now. The Kapitan was sweeping the horizon on either side of his target.

"The poor fool. He forgets that he is alone. For once—just for once—I have a British escort in my sights, and I do not have to worry whether another is about to attack me. I have prayed for this so many times. Port ten, Coxswain, let her come round slowly. Ah—das ist gut—I enjoy myself. Stand by to fire. Fire six!" The boat lurched as the torpedo sped on its way. (that is good)

"Torpedo running," Braun, the hydrophone operator, reported.

"Fire five!" the Kapitan ordered, and again the boat lurched.

"Torpedo running," Braun repeated.

"Kunz, what is the length of run?"

"One minute forty-eight seconds, Herr Kapitan." Kunz held a stop-watch in his hand.

The Kapitan, his eyes glued to the periscope, answered: "Tell me when the first fish has been running for a minute."

"Jawohl, Herr Kapitan."

The tense-faced men gathered round the Kapitan in

50

the control room saw his braced legs and back stiffen
to rigidity, and heard an explosive "Du lieber Gott! (For the love of God!.)
He turns! He cannot see my torpedoes—but he turns
under full helm."

"One minute, Herr Kapitan."

"You fool! This is all your fault," the Kapitan exploded, burning up his rising chagrin with a return to
the original complaint.

The Executive Officer made a mental note that now
there would be no bombastic reports written on this
episode—and he smiled rather ruefully.

The Kapitan, watching the destroyer in the circular view of the periscope, saw that her bow was
pointing directly toward him; and before he had seen
the whole of her port side. She was still turning; as
much of her starboard side was visible as before there
had been of the port. The target was already moving
slowly to the *right* across the little black lines etched
on the glass of the periscope—and the torpedoes had
been fired with twenty-five degrees of *left* deflection.
He had missed.

Kunz opened his mouth to tell his Kapitan that the
first torpedo should be arriving. He caught Schwachofer's eye and hesitated. Slowly Schwachofer shook
his head and dropped the corners of his mouth. Kunz
tried hard but only succeeded in irritating the two
"Vons." Schwachofer held that the freemasonry of the
sea service should override all other considerations.
He was sorry for Kunz.

Von Stolberg whipped the periscope down. The hiss
it made as it slid into its well sounded as if its pride
was hurt. "Dive to eighty meters, Herr Oberleutnant.
Silent routine. Warn Engineer Kritz that we shall be
shortly attacked with depth charges."

In the last second before he lowered his periscope the Kapitan had seen the destroyer's bows begin to turn back to starboard—toward him. The turn had not, then, been a lucky chance but a deliberately timed and carefully thought-out maneuver. Such a possibility had not, until the last moment, appeared to be credible—and he realized for the first time that he was up against another brain. In all his previous experience a target had been simply a target. The lumbering shapes of merchantmen had proceeded sedately along a straight line. His machines had calculated the angles. He had given the orders to fire when certain prerequisites had been observed. Then, so long as his trained guesses at the target's course, speed, and range were reasonably accurate—and provided the temperamental torpedoes ran correctly—hits were obtained: hits that in the fullness of time brought congratulatory letters and iron crosses. That this well-known procedure was not functioning now was an uneasy thought; and it was quickly followed by one that was worse. Suppose the opposing brain were better than his own? For the first time in his life von Stolberg saw death and knew it for what it could be.

"Asdic transmissions green one-six-five," Braun reported, spinning the polished wheel that directed the hydrophones. Before the Kapitan could acknowledge the information, he added: "closing. Propeller noises. Probably turbines, one-five-oh revolutions."

In the silent control room the waiting men, who hardly dared to breathe, could hear the sharp zip of the asdic transmissions that struck the U-boat's hull ten seconds apart. It was heard by them as the whisper of a whip about to be laid across their steel back.

BOOK TWO

Asdic Duel

06.35, Zone Time, Wednesday,
8 September.
Position 06° 23′ N. 33° 28′ W.

1

THE *Hecate* advanced upon her quarry. Circumstances had decided her Captain that he must attack up his adversary's tail. There was no time to work out on her beam, and he did not wish to risk another torpedo attack by delaying his first too long. In any case an alert U-boat, fighting a single escort, would nearly always present her opponent with a stern attack by continually turning away from his approach. He was not to know either the urgency that existed in von Stolberg's mind or the desperate attempts that that determined man would make in order to keep his rendezvous. The *Hecate's* Captain knew nothing of the time nor place, nor could he realize the efforts that must be made if the rendezvous was to be achieved with the last twenty-eight hours submerged.

The British captain was not entirely happy. Trained before the war in asdic trawlers, and until recently commanding a corvette, he was used to carrying out attacks by going into the asdic hut and there donning one set of headphones himself. In the destroyer, instead of leaving the bridge, he was expected to do the work with the aid of a loud-speaker. Mechanically the loud-speaker gave a faultless performance, but it had always seemed to him that slipping the headphones over his ears had the psychological effect of putting him in direct contact with the delicate instrument that was fixed to his ship's bottom. Accustomed to one method, he found that the new one, dictated by the larger ship, was irksome in the extreme. Not being gifted with a really musical ear, he had managed by practice to teach himself to detect the smallest alteration in the tonal qualities of the echo that came back from the submarine. Alterations of tone that, betraying a change of course on her part, would be used to form his own decisions. This affinity with his instrument he found to be much more difficult to achieve now that the sounds came to him through the voice of a loud-speaker.

"Steer two-oh-eight."

"Steer two-oh-eight." The First Lieutenant at his action station by the standard compass relayed his Captain's order to the wheelhouse. Here was cause for yet another vexation—the slight delay in time that relayed orders must cause, for he dared not imperil his hearing by mounting the raised plinth that surrounded the compass. To do so meant his leaving the sheltered corner of the bridge from whence he could best hear the loud-speaker. Another minor complaint, and one that did not in the early hours trouble him in any way, was that the Captain's chair, which he alone had the right to use (although he assumed correctly that every officer of the watch used it too during the

56

darkness of the night), was fixed beside the standard compass. At the moment he was far too excited to consider its use; but if the battle should be a prolonged one, it would have afforded rest to tired limbs.

"Echo bearing two-oh-nine. Going away. Range fifteen hundred," announced the voice pipe from the asdic cabinet.

"Steer two-oh-nine."

He had a well-trained ship. Everything should be functioning smoothly—as indeed it was. He crossed to a conical metal table on the port side of the bridge and raised the lid. This allowed him to view the automatic plot below. At the moment all he could see was the head and shoulders of the navigator.

"Stand back, Pilot, and let me have a look," he said. On the deck below him the navigator straightened his back. There the battle was laid out in colored chalk. Red for the enemy, blue for his own ship.

"Echo bearing two-one-oh. Going away. Range thirteen hundred."

The navigator glanced inquiringly at his Captain.

"Plot it," the Captain told him, and to the First Lieutenant: "Steer two-one-oh. I wonder where I've heard that course before!" He glanced again at the plot. The navigator, who had hurriedly marked up yet another red cross, was standing back again.

"He certainly is wedded to his course," the Captain remarked.

"Double echoes, the first at twelve hundred, the second at a thousand," the asdic voice pipe said.

The Captain crossed to the voice pipe. "Don't lose the further one. Try and give the plot the range of both." He went back to the plot.

"Asdic reports 'double echoes.' The wily bird may have slipped a *pillenwerfer*. I've told them to give you both ranges. If you find the first one stationary, tell me at once, and I'll tell asdic to disregard it."

"Echoes two-one-oh degrees. The first range seven hundred, the second nine hundred. First echo stationary," the navigator said.

"Thank you, Pilot," and to the asdic: "Disregard the first echo. It's a pill."

So the German thought to fox him with that old game. It was one that every escort knew well. The bubble-making canister would temporarily give off an echo that was very similar to one made by a submarine. The Germans had hoped that behind this underwater smoke screen they could slip away. But accurate plotting had detected the device.

"Submarine echo bearing two-one-oh seven hundred."

The Captain noted the word "submarine" inserted in the report to show that the asdic officer knew the position. Hopkins certainly had his head screwed on correctly.

The *Hecate* bore down on her quarry. There was no last-minute dash or excitement. She did not tear into her prey with a wave leaping from either bow. At fifteen knots she trundled over the sea, much as the popular conception of a grizzly bear—rolling slightly and with plodding gait.

"Echo bearing two-one-oh. Five hundred. Interrogative depth settings, sir?" the asdic queried.

"I'd like to wait as long as I can before deciding on the depth. Set the charges to seventy-five feet. If I want to make a last-minute alteration, I may do so," the Captain replied.

Hopkins in the asdic hut turned the dial that repeated the seventy-five-foot depth-setting order to the depth-charge party aft. That would start the ratings there in a hurried scamper to set the correct depth on the ten charges that were being prepared.

The *Hecate's* Captain had no idea of the depth of his enemy; and the charges must be released correctly in plan and also set to fire at the right depth. The enemy could be anything up to six hundred feet below the surface. He would get some idea from the last contact with the U-boat. The asdic beam did not go straight down. Beneath the ship there was a cone of silence, the sides at an angle of sixty degrees. Within this cone the U-boat could not be detected. The farther away it was when it passed inside the cone, the deeper it must be. This presented still another problem for the Captain. When two escorts were present, the one attacking could estimate the depth with some accuracy and the other ship would then have an idea what depth to set on her charges when the time came for her own attack.

"Two-one-oh; four hundred."

If only another escort was with him! Someone to whom he could signal, *"Come over here, and help me with this one."* Another escort would enable him to break what he guessed would be an endless series of stern attacks. By working out on the beam the other ship would have come in across the submarine's track as soon as the disturbance of his own bursting charges had subsided. Already he half regretted his grandiloquent words to the Doctor the night before. This "Chesapeake and Shannon," single-ship fight was going to be a problem.

"Two-one-oh; three hundred."

He must think of the depth-charge position too. He'd got to sink the enemy in ten tries—or if not sink her, then to force her to the surface, so that gun or ram could finish her off. Already he considered that she had shown too much spirit to hope for a surrender. The *Hecate's* full complement of charges was one hundred and ten. When they had been with the convoy, ten charges had been spent on an attack on what was afterward classified as a nonsubmarine target. That left her only a hundred. Two ships would have had at least two hundred depth charges and would have been able to lay them more correctly.

"Lost contact ahead, sir," said the asdic hut.

"Set charges to one fifty feet," the Captain ordered.

Hopkins spun the wheel of the repeater. At the same moment he pressed the buzzer that was the "Stand By" for the depth-charge firing party mustered on the afterdeck.

Mr. Grain, Commissioned Torpedo Gunner in charge of the depth-charge parties, heard the buzzer.

"Stand by charges," he shouted. Then his ear caught the higher, smaller note of the repeater bell, and out of the corner of his eye he saw the repeater begin to tick. "Set charges to one fifty," he yelled and dashed to help set as many as he could in the short time available.

The procedure was now automatic. No one in the *Hecate* could know what the submarine was doing, for the destroyer was passing over the U-boat. They only knew what the boat had been doing. This knowledge had been put on the instruments that would fire the charges by electrical impulses.

Two charges were automatically released from the

after rails. Leading Torpedoman Ellis was resetting the depth on the last of the ten charges. To steady himself he put his hand on one of the rails. The heavy depth charge rolled over it, shattering his wrist. He was assisted forward to the sick bay swearing softly and continuously. The accident was not known on the bridge until after the attack.

The depth-charge throwers barked, sending their charges wobbling through the sunlit air. Two on each side, four in all. Two more pairs of death-dealing canisters rolled from her rails. The eggs had been laid by the bird of death, but there was no time for the depth-charge crews to watch the explosions. Already Grain was lashing his men with his tongue to get the throwers reloaded and the rails refilled, for it was a point of honor in all the ocean escorts to reload at once. Two minutes was considered a bad time by a smart ship, where the difference between a good and a bad time was measured in seconds.

High on the bridge, expectant faces peered aft. The rising sun into which they looked warmed their tanned skins. The water astern shimmered golden and was broken by the wide, dark arrow of the *Hecate's* wash. Then the explosions came—the bursting of the first charges, followed by more surface-shaking explosions, until the watchers wondered how anything made by man could possibly withstand the terrible shock.

The silence after the last explosions was almost palpable, and for a while men lowered their voices as in the presence of the dead.

2

Von Stolberg turned to his Executive Officer. "Heini, you have the course and depth?"

"Jawohl, Herr Kapitan. Course two-one-oh. Speed four knots, depth eighty meters."

"That is good. Oberleutnant von Holem," he said over his shoulder. There was no need to raise his voice in the confined quarters of the control room.

"Ja, Herr Kapitan?"

Von Holem stood up from the chart table and as a mark of respect to his Kapitan he stood stiffly to attention. It was not only a personal gesture from a junior to a senior. It expressed all the pride of a man who considered both himself and the man to whom he offered this deference to be of a race apart.

"Otto," the Kapitan said, "let us consider the rendezvous. You had star sights last night?"

"Ja, Herr Kapitan—but not so good. The cloud was low and the boat rolling heavily. Also the spray interfered greatly with the sextant."

The Kapitan's face had clouded during this recital. He was on the point of complaining when the navigator went on: "But I had perfect sights this morning."

"Ah, that is good indeed. I did not know that you had taken them. Where are we then?" He moved to stand before the table.

"Here, Herr Kapitan." The navigator's sharp pencil indicated the little cross on the white chart. Diagonally across the paper a black line was traced. There were many little crosses—very near to the line. Some were on one side of it, some on the other. The cross to which von Holem pointed was the last one, and the one that was the nearest to the big, heavily marked circle where the line ended.

"How far to go?" the Kapitan asked.

"At six hours two minutes zone time this morning we had yet to make ninety-six miles, Herr Kapitan."

"So that at four knots we shall be in position at six o'clock tomorrow morning."

"That is so."

"That leaves us still six hours to spare before noon tomorrow."

"Provided our course and speed are maintained."

"Yes, Otto, yes," the other answered softly, "provided as you say, Herr Oberleutnant, that our course and speed are maintained." His voice grew hard. "A thousand curses on this Britisher!" The two men looked at each other. His navigator was closer to the Kapitan than anyone else in the ship. Their families knew each other and cousins had intermarried. The Kapitan's voice dropped to a whisper. "Otto, how could *you* have been so silly?" The emphasis on the word "you" not only made a distinction between Otto and the others but also showed that the others had been presumed to be capable of silliness all along.

"I don't know. It was just one of those things. A fool's paradise."

The Kapitan turned away wearily. The control room was a huddle of well-trained men carrying out precise duties. For a while he had even forgotten to listen to the zip-zip of the asdic transmission. He must gather up the reins ready for the evasive action that he would take.

"Stand by *pillenwerfer*," he ordered. He did not really expect it to perform the function for which it had been designed, but he hoped that it might confuse the issue, and at least it would give him the measure of the enemy that he was up against.

Müller had come from aft, having secured the stern caps of the tubes. The forward tubes could be reloaded when the U-boat was submerged, even though it took a long time, and the boat must be on an even keel if the heavy torpedoes were to be eased successfully into the tubes. But to reload the stern tubes they must surface, and that, under the present conditions, Müller knew to be impossible. Now, hearing the order to release a *pillenwerfer*, he went to the release gear and put his hand on the lever.

"Wait," the Kapitan said to him, and to Braun at the hydrophones: "Braun, can you give me any idea of the range?"

"It is very difficult, Herr Kapitan. The enemy is astern of us, and there is much interference from the noise of our own propellers. He comes closer all the time. I think he is about one thousand meters."

The Kapitan shrugged his shoulders and signaled to Müller. Müller's hand came down. There was a slight but audible hiss as the *pillenwerfer* was ejected from its canister. "Let me know if the range increases," von Stolberg said to Braun.

"Zum Befehl, Herr Kapitan."

They waited in tense silence. The seconds ticked by, became minutes. "Well?" the Kapitan asked.

"The range still decreases, Herr Kapitan."

"As I feared."

Von Stolberg moved back to the center of the control room. To be depth-charged was, for him and for most of his crew, no new experience. The Kapitan had been at sea in command as long as, if not longer than, any other surviving U-boat Kapitan, and he was far too clever and experienced to be caught napping. If his sinkings were less than the score that had been credited to many others, at least he was still alive— and they were dead.

"I will wait until the destroyer is almost above me. Then I will turn to port to the reverse course. Full speed during the turn on the starboard engine. Then reduce to four knots. We will release two *pillenwerfer* as soon as the boat has turned, and hold the reverse course of oh-three-oh degrees for fifteen minutes. It is possible that we may shake him off. If we are successful, we will at the end of fifteen minutes alter course ninety degrees to starboard to one-two-oh degrees for a further forty-five minutes and then resume our course of two-one-oh degrees. That will mean"—he turned to the navigator—"that we shall end up on a parallel course three miles southeast of our present one. We shall lose almost one hour and a half. It is a great pity, but I do not see how it can be helped."

"It cuts down the time in hand to four hours and a half."

The Kapitan nodded. "I know—but I would like to lose this fellow. He is too close to that which he should not see."

Kunz, who had listened throughout this speech, had felt that the Kapitan should have finished with a *"Heil Hitler!"* He was used to this form of exhortation and found the lack of it discouraging. Neither von Stolberg nor von Holem ever replied to his *"Heils"* when they were at sea because they were born of people who had been persons before his hero had come. Schwachofer, too, was far too cosmopolitan to indulge in the salute, although Kunz was aware of his sympathy when he himself was in trouble with the "vons." There were deep and undeniable schisms among the officers of *U-121;* and among the men, too, there were both Nazis and those who were just Germans.

All in the boat could hear the throbbing beat of the propellers. It grew louder, like a freight train coming toward one through a tunnel.

"Port thirty. Full ahead starboard. Steady on oh-three-oh."

The waiting men felt the boat begin to turn. The hum of the engines increased. In the dark depths she began to circle and to retrace her steps.

The destroyer ran on blind, to drop her charges.

3

S WEEP ASTERN," the *Hecate's* Captain gave the order to the asdic cabinet.

"Sweep astern, sir," Hopkins' voice repeated back. Then: "Very confused echoes, sir. It looks as if it will take some time for the disturbance to subside."

"I'll open the range—it will give us more chance."

The *Hecate* moved away from the circle of disturbed water. In three minutes she had left it fifteen hundred yards astern. There was still no echo that was recognizable as one that could have come from a U-boat.

Mystified, chagrined, and worried, the Captain brought his ship around to head back toward the position of the attack. The turn took a further three minutes. Had he but known it, the U-boat, which could turn more quickly than the destroyer, was now making off at her best speed behind the curtain of disturbed water, to which she had added her own two *pillen-*

werfer. The boat was already sixteen hundred yards on the other side of the disturbance and out of asdic range.

"No contact," the asdic cabinet announced.

"Carry out an all-around sweep."

His enemy had eluded him. He had expected to find the real submarine echo coming out of the confusion of the bursting charges as a headland stands out of a fog. A hard outline appearing where before there had only been confused vapors. The U-boat must have turned and gone elsewhere, for the Captain was not so sanguine as to imagine that his one attack had achieved complete and instant destruction. He was a very worried man.

He was even more upset when he heard of the damage done to Ellis' wrist. For this accident he blamed himself. He had asked too much in ordering a resetting of depths, once the automatic firing device had been set to function. He knew how angry he himself would have been if one of his officers in a practice drill had been the cause of a like accident occurring. Action obviously excused a great deal, but before the bar of his own judgment he found himself arraigned and condemned.

The *Hecate* was now steaming through the disturbance of her attack. The asdic beam, groping like the finger of a blind man, probed the sea around her.

"No contact, sir," the asdic hut announced.

"Try again."

"Sweep all around, sir," Hopkins repeated.

The Captain went to the plot and bent over it.

"He's given us the slip, Pilot. I'll go to a position four miles to starboard of the attack and carry out an all-around sweep there. I'll go fast with the asdic housed."

"Aye aye, sir."

The asdic hut said, "No contact, sir."

"Stop transmitting. House the asdic," and to the First Lieutenant: "Port twenty steer two-eight-oh. Three hundred revolutions."

The ship heeled over sharply, both under the impetus of the rudder and the thrust of the big propellers that were now striving to work the ship's speed up to thirty knots. She vibrated all over like an excited horse. The pitometer log ticked ever faster as her speed grew. A waft of hot funnel gas was blown round the bridge. The wake began to form a long, creaming line astern.

The Captain went back to the plot. "Let me know when we are five hundred yards short of the position."

He climbed up on the plinth around the binnacle so that the cool morning wind should blow against his face. He felt tired and hungry and dispirited— but he could never show what he felt. Only nine minutes elapsed before the navigator called from the plot.

"Five hundred yards to go, sir."

"One-five-oh revolutions. Steer two-one-oh degrees."

The *Hecate's* speed fell as quickly as it had been called for. Her Captain spoke to the asdic hut. "Lower the asdic. Commence transmission. Carry out an all-around sweep."

He went back to the view plot. "Pilot, if we have no luck this side, I'll try the other. I'm sure that he'll try and get back to his old course of two-one-oh. I think that if he gives that up, he's almost as much a beaten man as if he'd been sunk. Lay this off for me. Give the U-boat a turn to port from the diving position; then allow for him steering a reciprocal course to his old one for fifteen minutes at six knots. Then let him turn for forty minutes to a course of one-two-oh at four knots, and then bring him back to his old two-one-oh track."

The asdic interrupted: "No contact, sir."

To the asdic: "Try again," and then turning once more to the navigator: "I'll want a course and speed to intercept—something in the twenty-eight-knot class. He'll not try to torpedo us at that speed."

"Aye aye, sir," The navigator bent busily to his task, pausing every now and then to consult his slide rule. The Captain watched for a moment, then paused to light a cigarette.

"No contact, sir," Hopkins reported.

"Very well. Stop transmitting. Raise the asdic." The Captain hurried back to the plot. "Ready with that course yet, Pilot?"

"One-five-two degrees at twenty-nine knots, sir."

"Good lad! Let me know when we are five hundred from the point of interception," and to the First Lieutenant: "Steer one-five-two. Two-nine-oh revolutions."

Once more the *Hecate* heeled and throbbed. As soon as she was settled to her course, the bow wave began to rise. The stern sank and a plume of white froth rose fanlike along her wake, where the terrific disturbance created by thirty thousand horsepower was dissipated in the ocean. The Captain, looking aft at the wake-whitening astern, saw his steward leave the after deckhouse and brace himself against the roll as he hurried forward. In one hand he was carrying a sling. His passage was a series of zigzags along the deck, and once he had to pause to hold on. Soon he was mounting the long ladders that led to the bridge.

The Captain went to the chart table.

"Your breakfast, sir."

"Robins, how did you know that I have just fifteen minutes in which I've a chance to eat?"

"That's just luck, sir. It's eight o'clock. Your breakfast time, sir. Nothing unusual about it at all. There, sir, bacon and scrambled egg. Reconstituted. All we've got left now, sir. Though it's not too bad, really."

He poured out a cup of coffee and stood it carefully among the pencils and rubber in the tray at the back of the table. Secretly the Captain went in terror of Robins, who treated him in much the same way a nannie will treat her young charges. When the Captain gave a dinner party in harbor, he was always half expecting, until the guests arrived, that Robins would inquire into the state of his hands or ask if he had washed behind the ears.

The Captain, seizing knife and fork, hastily began to put food in his mouth. Meals must be snatched, and the sooner the business of eating was over the better. He turned to the First Lieutenant. "Number One, I don't know what we'll do about the officers' breakfast. I think the stewards had better carry the food around. We can send a quarter of the men at a time from each position to breakfast, but they'll have to come back at the double if we sound the alarm. It may take us some time to find the fellow again."

"I don't know how he managed to disappear like that."

"He turned right around and left us only the smell. He's a cunning one all right. He turns more quickly than we do. Now if I had my old corvette, I could turn more quickly than he and prevent him always offering me his tail. But then of course, if we were a corvette, he'd just surface and run away from us. We're better to be what we are, if we are fighting single-ship. If you have speed you have length, and that means you can't turn."

The Captain finished his meal and took the cup of coffee in his hands.

"Forebridge." The voice came from the plot.

"Forebridge."

"Five hundred to go, sir."

"Thank you, Pilot."

The Captain nodded to the First Lieutenant. "Slow her down, Number One, and bring her round to two-one-oh." Then to the asdic: "Lower asdic, commence transmission."

"All around, sir?"

"Yes, all-around sweep."

Once more the ping of the asdic was heard on the bridge as the ship's speed dropped. Ping—Ping—Ping—PING—PONG.

"Good God, we're almost on top of him!"

The asdic was calling excitedly. "Captain, sir. Captain, sir."

"Stop jabbering, Hopkins! I can hear it—fine on the port bow. What's the range?"

"Four hundred. Bearing one-four-oh."

"Have you time to attack?"

"Yes, sir."

"Carry on. Set charges, two hundred and fifty feet. Stand by charges."

"Aye aye, sir. Target drawing right."

"Steer one-eight-oh."

"Range three hundred"—followed immediately by: "Lost contact ahead, sir."

The Captain pursed his lips. The whole episode was pure luck. Given that the deduction was correct, it was reasonable to suppose that contact would be regained somewhere within four square miles of where the *Hecate* then was. But to find himself suddenly over the U-boat was like finding a pin in a haystack by pricking himself with it. The attack had been far too hastily conceived to have any real chance of success. But luck might be on their side. To stop the charges from being fired—or to let them go? The seconds ticked by. If the pattern was fired—ten charges would go—and there would be ten less. Crossing his fingers, the Captain did not countermand the order.

The *Hecate* shivered as the charges exploded.

4

THE CHARGES that burst from the *Hecate's* first attack had jolted and jarred the U-boat. But bursting at least a hundred feet above her, and with the center of the pattern well on her starboard beam, they were no worse than many others that had been delivered against her in previous forays.

U-121 had turned rapidly and was retracing her steps. The noise of the destroyer's propellers was dying away—had gone. Her men could still sense, rather than hear, the swish of the asdic's whip. But it reached them only through the disturbed water of the explosion, and they felt that a curtain protected them and their boat. Soon even this was lost to unaided ears, even when they were pressed to the hull of the boat, and only Braun with his delicate instruments could hear the transmissions from the British ship.

"Half ahead, four knots," the Kapitan ordered when fifteen minutes had passed. "Steer one-two-oh."

The whirr of the motors eased. The little vibration that there had been died away. The boat stole stealthily forward, suspended in a dim world above one that was darker yet—and cold as death.

Braun called the control room from his voice pipe.

"Herr Kapitan, the British transmissions have stopped and I have heard fast but distant propellers. They are going away, Herr Kapitan. I think the destroyer has gone somewhere very fast."

Von Stolberg thought quickly. It seemed indeed as if he had been successful in shaking off the enemy. At least temporarily. But why had the destroyer suddenly moved away? It was at variance both to the drill that he himself had previously experienced and to that which was confirmed by other U-boat captains. In general the Germans would criticize those who hunted them, saying that they stayed so long in one spot, going around and around, that a determined and careful man could slip away. Von Stolberg was enough of a realist to recognize that it was a one-sided statement, because obviously those who didn't get away could make no comment. They were either dead or prisoners of war.

Either the British Captain was working some scheme of his own or something might have occurred up in the sun and air above that had drawn him off. Could it be that the *Cecilie* was early at her rendezvous—that, cruising in the area, she had unwittingly come across the destroyer attacking the U-boat that had been sent to meet her? Even now the success of the whole operation could be at stake—for although the armed merchant-cruiser could certainly sink the destroyer, she would never catch her if the latter should decide to keep out of gun range and wireless to the British Admiralty for assistance. The raider's Captain would know that as well as anyone. He would pretend to be a harmless merchantman, and try to lure the destroyer within range of his hidden guns in order to deal her a lethal blow before ever she could make a signal. Von Stolberg wondered what ruse he'd try. The idea of asking for a doctor presented itself to his fertile imagination. He liked that idea. The sentimental English would fall easily for that one. He could imagine the destroyer lying stopped and close alongside the merchantman. The boat being lowered—swinging in the falls ready to be slipped. The destroyer's crew would be lining the rails, watching. No one would suspect the supposed merchantman—until too late. He would like to be the German Captain at that moment.

"Time to turn to course two-one-oh, Herr Kapitan." It was the navigator speaking. With an effort von Stolberg returned from his visionary fancy.

"Very well."

He heard the order given. But was it "very well"? Was the course the best for him? He was free of the Britisher, who had either gone away to look at something else or had hopelessly misjudged the German's actions. If the Kapitan kept on steering toward the southeast, the chances of being found were very remote indeed. For even if the destroyer did come down that way, he would hear the transmission of her asdic long before she was close enough to detect an echo, and he would be able to avoid her. At extreme range a U-boat could nearly always avoid a single ship. An escort group, searching in line abreast, was a very different matter from the lone hunter. To the southeast lay safety, and who would ever be able to question seriously the wisdom of his decision? One of his paramount duties was to see to the safety of his ship. Would honor be satisfied if he steered to the southeast until dusk and then surfaced to go on to the rendezvous on his diesels? If he adopted that course, he thought he could just make it in time. But it would be very very tight, and he would have nothing to spare if anything were to go wrong. A sailor must always have something in hand of time or speed, and he would have neither.

"Very well, Herr Oberleutnant. Steer two-one-oh." His mouth was compressed. Deep lines had etched themselves on his pale face. Forming a triangle, the lines ran from the corners of his nose to the edge of his lips. If he had instinctively drawn himself up, as though standing to attention on the parade ground, his men paid no attention—they were far too busy watching their instruments. In making his decision he had performed his duty as it presented itself to him. To make the rendezvous was vital, both to his personal honor and the success of the Fatherland—for the prize was colossal. If he were to achieve his object, the photocopies of the precious ciphers would be in the hands of the High Command at least fourteen days earlier than the originals brought back by the *Cecilie,* and, with luck, a day or two before they were due to be brought into force. Ahead of the surface ship lay a long dangerous and circuitous route that would take her from the warm Equator to the cold mists of the northern passage beyond Iceland. Often she would be forced to dodge backward and forward, for when sighted by any other ship she must pretend to be a fast merchantman sailing independently between the American continent and the British Isles. Her chances of escaping the vigilance of the Allied navies and their infernally efficient Coastal Command aircraft were by no means sure. It was quite possible that she would never reach Bremen at all; and in that case the copies taken back to Brest by *U-121* would be the only record.

However lucky, or unlucky, the *Cecilie* might be in her dash for the Denmark strait and the northern route, it would be at least five weeks before she could hope to make a German harbor. He, von Stolberg, could deliver the documents in three weeks. Two vital weeks would be saved—two weeks during which the Allied naval messages would be deciphered as readily by the Reich as by her enemies, who would still think that many hours or days must elapse before their complicated ciphers could be broken down and their messages read. The effect of the speedily acquired knowledge would be of immediate benefit, and the damage that might be inflicted on the enemy would be enormous. It could even be catastrophic.

At all costs he, Peter von Stolberg, would make the rendezvous. Somehow he would outwit the Britisher who seemed to be a man of a mercurial twist of mind. Temporarily he was free of him. Once again the Kapitan wondered why, after such a painstaking chase through the night—an operation that his professional ability could recognize and approve—the destroyer had suddenly taken itself off at high speed. Putting himself in his enemy's place, he envisaged a slow, thorough appraisal of all the factors, and the final production of a carefully devised search plan that would have kept the destroyer going round and round the same spot in ever-widening circles for the rest of the day.

He was more than ever sure that his decision had been the right one.

It was also a decision that had brought with it a sense of self-congratulation, and that in its turn engendered self-confidence. The latter condition was, he knew, a most necessary one for a U-boat commander —for a lack of confidence in his own ability to outwit the enemy was the equivalent of a lack of nerve. But there was something else that he would have found incapable of definition, for he worked and planned by inbred instinct and not by introspection. It was not his duty to his Führer—whom privately he still thought of as Herr Schickelgruber—that had helped him to his decision. It was not even the loyalty he owed to the submarine command in general, and to Grand Admiral Dönitz in particular. It went further back, into the dim but heroic German past.

Had Kunz had the thinking to do, he would have ended with the words, *"Heil Hitler."* In a like case Schwachofer would have thought, *"Heil dem Vaterland."* (hail the fatherland) Deep within himself the Kapitan's real self had whispered, *"Heil von Stolberg."*

The Kapitan bent his face to the voice pipe that led to the hydrophone cabinet. "Braun, can you hear anything?"

"Nothing, Herr Kapitan. Absolutely nothing."

What could the Britisher be up to? He was very tempted to go to periscope depth and take a look round. If the enemy had gone, he was quite safe. If the destroyer should return at anything like the speed

79

at which it had left, then the hydrophone would detect it when it was at least four miles away.

To Schwachofer he said, "Bring her up to fourteen meters. I wish to use the periscope."

The compressed air hissed as the water was expelled from the ballast tanks. The needle of the depth gauge rose quickly, then steadied for a moment as it touched twenty meters. Here the final trim was adjusted until the boat was quite level before the needle began a steady creep past nineteen, eighteen, to fourteen meters.

"Fourteen meters. Depth steady," Schwachofer reported.

"Good." Von Stolberg appreciated the quiet efficiency of his junior. Whatever happened, Schwachofer never permitted his emotions to show outwardly.

Once more the periscope rose smoothly from its well. One hand-grip controlled an angling mirror that allowed the sky to be searched. Instinctively the Kapitan carried out the anti-aircraft search that years of training under North Atlantic conditions had laid down as the first protective glance on surfacing—afterward he would look for the initially less dangerous surface ship.

But neither in the sky above nor on the surface could he see anything. No mast that waved above a rolling hull broke the horizon—a horizon that, now wind and sea were decreasing, was becoming hard and firm and only very slightly notched by waves. The thought crossed the Kapitan's mind that he might surface and try to run away on the diesels. He had already been dived for two hours. With even a few minutes on the engines he could refresh the air in the boat, replace the charge in the batteries that he had used, and put a few more miles between himself and the destroyer. In the bright light of day he would see her at least as soon as she saw him—possibly ten miles away or even more. At that distance the surface craft might well fail to gain asdic contact.

While he stayed down below, his horizon was limited by the height of his periscope above the water and was not much more than five miles. Fully surfaced, it was fifteen miles. At best such a course might lead to his escape; at worst it would give him two more hours submerged on the following day.

"Prepare to surface."

"Herr Kapitan, Herr Kapitan!" The voice was Braun's from the hydrophone cabinet.

"Answer it, Otto," the Kapitan said, his eye still glued to the slowly revolving periscope. He was aware of a hurried and excited colloquy behind him. "What is it?" He took his eyes from the periscope.

"Herr Kapitan, Braun reports high-speed propellers, distant, getting nearer."

The Kapitan left the periscope and pushed past von Holem to speak down the tube himself.

"How fast, Braun?"

"Very fast indeed, Herr Kapitan. I have never heard faster."

"What bearing?"

"On the starboard beam."

Back at the periscope, he swung it round to the starboard bearing and sank his forehead to rest against the thick rubber pad.

"Gott in Himmel!" In the center of the horizon two white plumes of water were visible. Between them swayed the destroyer's delicate mast and pale gray upperworks. It was useless to try to fire torpedoes at a destroyer traveling at that speed. Angrily he pushed the button that sent the periscope down into its well.

"Emergency dive to eighty meters."

"Jawohl, Herr Kapitan. Emergency dive to eighty meters," Schwachofer repeated.

The boat dipped steeply by the bow, and the engine hum increased. Schwachofer was flooding the forward tanks first in order to increase the angle of dive and make it easier for the propellers to send her hurtling into the depths. The valves would be shut off in the reverse order so that she would steady up on an even keel. The officer was—and had to be—an artist at catching her in her dizzy plunge downward; one false move on his part and she would go on down to a depth that would crush even her strong hull.

With one hand grasping the now-housed periscope to steady himself and with the other on the edge of Kunz's plotting table, von Stolberg swore softly and fluently to himself. How the devil could you fight a madman like this? Madmen were more dangerous than even the most skillful of men—because it was impossible to gauge what they would do next.

"Can you hear any asdic transmissions?" he asked Braun.

"No, Herr Kapitan."

That seemed reasonable, for what he had heard and read of the Allied asdic assured him that it could not be used above certain speeds. What then was in the British Captain's mind? It was more than possible that the destroyer would overshoot him and go rocketing off over the other horizon. If it boded a day of alarms and excursions, at least it was better than being continuously tailed.

The boat was leveling off, and her motors were eased back to give her the slower speed of four knots now that they had done their job and driven her down.

"Silent routine," he gave the order. This would put the hydroplanes, which like horizontal rudders controlled her depth, into hand control, so that the motors that worked them at other times would not add to the noise.

All in the boat could now hear the drumming of the propellers. It was a sustained rumble, ever growing in volume. Louder and louder it grew, until the ear, accustomed to the continually increasing racket, was shocked to hear the noise decreasing. Could she have passed beyond them and be going away? No need to ponder the problem seriously. The noise still came from the starboard beam. They did not need the hydrophone to tell them that. The noise was dying, fading.

And then, with a crack that made even the most hardened and experienced stiffen, the asdic's lash fell on the iron shell that contained them. An agonized whisper swept through the boat as the men simultaneously released their breaths.

Du lieber Gott, the Kapitan thought. On my beam at four hundred meters. No time to turn. The surprise for the destroyer will be great. If he attacks now, he has a chance to sink me. Perhaps he will not have the time. Perhaps he will run over me and get contact the other side. I will be ready for that. In the hurry he is likely to fire later rather than sooner. I will turn to starboard so that when he has crossed over me he will have my stern to look at.

"Hard astarboard—full ahead. Steer two-eight-oh."

The faster he could close with the destroyer, the less time she would have to prepare her attack.

The beat of propellers sounded overhead. He could sense that his men instinctively bent their heads. The seconds ticked by. The rumbling note of a depth charge was near enough in all conscience—if only it was no worse.

But it was! The *Hecate's* starboard throwers had hurled two charges fifty yards onto one side of her track. The heavy one, sinking more quickly than the light one, exploded beneath the U-boat. The light one exploded above her. Although both were just beyond the range of lethal damage, the shock wave between the two was appalling in intensity. It felt as if the boat had been picked up by a giant hand and thrown upon a concrete floor. Every single thing in her was flung up and down by the repeated waves. The lights went out, and in the semidarkness the little emergency lights, no bigger than flashlight bulbs, cast an eerie glow. The floor was littered and slippery with tiny fragments of shattered glass. A frostlike mantle was now all that remained of the many glass fronts to all the hundreds of dials that lined the control room.

The boat heaved and porpoised through the depths, while Schwachofer and his aides struggled desperately to regain control of her. Like a bubble in a spirit level, her trim swung backward and forward. Panting, with sweat pouring from their bodies, her crew fought for her life and theirs.

5

B Y THE time the effect of her exploding depth charges had ceased to deafen the asdic, the *Hecate's* Captain heard the joyful report from the asdic cabinet.

"Contact astern. Bearing green one-seven-oh. Range five hundred. Opening fast."

With both contestants moving in opposite directions, the range would increase at over six hundred yards a minute. It was therefore imperative to turn the destroyer to the opposite course without delay.

"Starboard thirty, steer three-oh-oh."

The *Hecate* heeled sharply. Her stern, swinging around in a great arc, crossed out every ripple on the sea and left it smooth as satin on the inside of the turn; while on the other, the ship's side skidded into the waves, and their tops fell aboard her.

"Green one-five-oh; green nine-oh; green seven-oh; green three-oh; green one-oh." The asdic reported steadily.

"Midships. Steady on three-oh-oh."

"Red oh-five," the asdic said. "Bearing two-nine-five. Range seventeen hundred. Submarine. Going away."

The Captain realized that he had barely turned in time. A minute—two minutes more—and the U-boat would have been free again. He crossed to the view plot. "What did it look like, Pilot?"

"If the depth was anywhere near right, the starboard thrower should have given him a nasty shaking, sir."

"I hope it did."

"Will you attack again, sir?" the First Lieutenant asked.

"Let's give him one more while he's feeling shaky. Only eight patterns left—that's the real rub. After this attack there will be only seven."

The *Hecate* was once more faced with a stern attack. Her last one had been from across the U-boat's beam, but she could hardly hope to achieve such surprise again.

Rolling heavily, with the old swell on her beam, the destroyer, with waddling gait, carried out her third attack. Again the charges were set to two hundred and fifty feet, although contact had been lost ahead when they were farther away. The Captain would again have liked to alter the pattern at the last moment, but the memory of Ellis' crushed hand had held him back until there was no time to relay his orders to stop the pattern being fired. Seventy charges left.

"Contact astern bearing one-five-oh, range five hundred," the asdic announced.

A mercy that at any rate they were still in contact. As usual he went to the view plot. "Well, Pilot?"

"The U-boat turned to port at the last moment, sir. He's back on his two-one-oh course, or I'm much mistaken."

"What a fool I am! Of course he'd turn one way or the other and no need to guess which! I should have kept out on his port side. Too late now. Better luck next time. That pattern won't have hurt him much."

What to do? To continue attacking this wily bird until all his ammunition was exhausted or to lay astern of him and just hold contact while he thought things over? Stewards were appearing on the bridge carrying plates of food for the officers. It was all rather like a gigantic school outing. He'd drop astern. In many ways he would have liked to lie on the U-boat's beam, about half a mile away, and steam gently along with it. But to do so was to risk a torpedo attack. The U-boat, he knew, was at the moment too far down to fire his torpedoes. But he might come up slowly until he was able to do so. The new U-boats carried torpedoes that could be angled to turn to a course at least ninety, and some said one hundred and twenty, degrees from the direction in which they were fired. Decidedly it would be better to tag along astern.

He went to the compass platform. "All right, Number One. I'll take her while you have your breakfast. I'm going to take station half a mile astern of him for a bit."

The *Hecate* settled down to wait, like a great dog at the bottom of a tree. The U-boat plodded on her course of two-one-oh degrees. Astern of her, with slow speed on her engines, lazily wallowed the destroyer, her men basking in the sunshine and going to their breakfast in watches. The bridge sweepers appeared and swept away the night's litter of cigarette papers, the wrappers of chocolate bars, and the extraordinary amount of real dust that would accumulate on the open bridge in the middle of the Atlantic. Every five minutes the asdic cabinet reported the range and bearing: "Bearing two-one-oh, range one thousand."

The Captain went down to his sea cabin for a shave. Afterward he went down to the sick bay to see Ellis.

"I'm sorry about that hand of yours."

"Me own fault, sir."

"Not entirely, Ellis. I asked a hell of a lot, to change the depth settings at the last moment."

"Will you sink the bastard, sir?"

"I hope so, Ellis."

"I hope so too, sir. I shouldn't feel at all bad about it if you do."

"I'll try and get you flown back as soon as we get into Freetown. The plastic surgeons at home are wonderful fellows."

"So I've heard, sir. Thank you, sir."

"What's your job in civvy-street, Ellis?"

"Wood-turner, sir."

"Oh!" The Captain had hoped he was in some measure making amends, but Ellis would never turn wood again. The plastic surgeons were only surgeons —not magicians.

"Well, don't let it get you down, Ellis."

"I won't let it do that, sir. Not so be as you sink yon bloody sub."

"I'll do my best, Ellis—so will the ship." The Captain went sadly back to the bridge.

On the bridge he noticed the tidy atmosphere at once.

"Well done, Number One. She looks a bit more like our *Hecate* now." How quickly a Captain had to change his manner.

The navigator, hearing his return, called him from the plot. "Permission to hand over plot to Sublieutenant Willis, sir, while I take my nine A.M. sight and wind the chronometer."

"Carry on, Pilot." Then to the First Lieutenant: "Number One, collect the Coxswain, the senior asdic rating, and Mr. Grain up here. I think we'll have a little conference."

"Aye aye, sir."

The navigator came on the bridge carrying his sextant and accompanied by a sailor with the deck watch in its brown mahogany case.

"As soon as you've shot your sun, Pilot, I want you to join my party and discuss the situation. I'm afraid we are in for a long, long battle," the Captain addressed the men who had gathered in a sheltered corner of the bridge. "I don't think I ever realized before at what a disadvantage a single destroyer is. The U-boat can turn more quickly than we can, and will always give us his stern to attack. We've already expended a third of our charges, and the U-boat need not surface for twenty-four hours. That is the crux of the position. In twenty-four hours, or thereabouts, he will have exhausted his air and, if I can't break his hull, at least I hope to shatter his nerve. Now that's a long battle and you can't keep on all the time.

89

Not you, Pilot, on the plot, nor you, Thomson, on the asdic, nor you, Coxswain, on the wheel. We may have to be on the top line at any moment—suddenly, and with very little warning. So I want you all to get somewhere comfortable near your own particular part of the ship, and sit down and rest. We've a lot of well-trained ratings, and they are quite capable of doing the routine jobs, so long as the first team is ready to take over in an emergency. It won't be exactly pleasant, but it will be a damn sight worse for the Hun. I've got seven patterns left and there are six watches before his twenty-four hours are up. We'll attack him at eleven-thirty, three-thirty, five-thirty, seven-thirty, eleven-thirty, three-thirty and the last one at dawn tomorrow. After a bit he'll get to know the drill; and my bet is that when he tumbles to what we've got in store for him, it will shake him as much as, if not more than, we will with our charges."

The *Hecate* replaced her sword in the sheath, but she kept her right hand firmly on the hilt.

6

IN THE dim light von Stolberg peered over Schwachofer's shoulder.

"What depth?" he asked.

"Hundred and ten—all the tanks are working correctly."

"We lost thirty meters."

"Ja, Herr Kapitan."

"Keep her steady at a hundred and ten until we've checked on the damage. If there is nothing serious I'll go deep to a hundred and fifty meters."

Von Stolberg's speech had not been made in his usual voice. Schwachofer noticed the change but made no comment. Even had he dared to make a personal remark to the very impersonal man who was his commanding officer, comment would have been superfluous. He wondered what his own voice sounded like, for his mouth was as dry as if he had marched across a desert.

Already the electricians were hurrying around the boat replacing the broken bulbs. The main fault in the lights was traced to a blown fuse on the main switchboard. When this had been replaced, the lighting was back to normal.

Most men in the boat were more upset by the sudden return of the light than by the thought of remaining in the dim emergency lighting, which had engendered a cosy atmosphere. In the return of current to the main bulbs, they were at once made freshly aware of the power of their enemy—for now the full extent of the ordeal through which their boat had passed could be seen and assessed. The cork insulation had been stripped in great irregular-shaped pieces from the plating. It covered everything—bunks, floor, and the men themsleves. Strips of it hung festooned among the pipes and valves that surrounded the control room. As a sample of what could happen to them, it was almost as unnerving as the explosion itself had been. There was not a gauge glass that had not been shattered, and the broken shards were everywhere, even on their own bodies.

Von Stolberg, turning sharply from the depth gauge, slipped on the glass-strewn deck. "Get this mess swept up," he spoke to Kunz, who put his head into the forward torpedo room and called to the petty officer there to send a man with a brush.

Slowly the Kapitan felt his nerves, which had seemed to turn to vibrating piano wires, relax. He had to admit that it was the most devastating blow that he had ever felt in his three years in the submarine service. Had he been able to realize it, there was no cause for surprise in that. The depth charges had exploded only just outside the critical distance. Six feet, even three feet closer, and mortal damage would almost surely have been done.

He went to the door of the hydrophone cabinet and looked in. "Your ears were not damaged, Braun?" he asked.

"No, Herr Kapitan. I had warning. When the first charge exploded I removed the headphones."

"That is good." It was not unknown for the hydrophone operators to have their hearing seriously impaired, for their instrument greatly magnified all sounds in the water. The Kapitan was therefore as much interested in his operator's ears as he was in the correct functioning of any other instrument in the boat. His query had been made solely for this reason. It was not that von Stolberg was a cruel man—he was just insensible to the feelings of others. He detested the thought of the cruelties that his brother Germans, the Nazis, were daily performing in the prison camps. It never crossed his mind that their activities were in any way connected with the von Stolbergs; and if anyone had suggested to him that he shared the responsibility, he would have been angered at such an insult.

"Can you hear anything?"

"Ja, Herr Kapitan. The destroyer is in contact astern. It is difficult to tell her range because she is blanketed by our own propellers. I fancy that she comes closer."

Otto Kritz, the engineer, was waiting for him.

"Well?"

"No material damage, Herr Kapitan."

"Safe to go to one hundred and fifty meters?"

"As far as I can ascertain, yes."

The Kapitan turned to Schwachofer. "Take her down to one hundred and fifty." It was unlikely that the British ship was in any way aware of the near-success of her last attack. The oil tanks, which at that depth would have immediately registered any puncture, were undamaged: thus there was no clue that would provide the destroyer's Captain with confirmation of the accuracy of his guess. However, now that the destroyer was attacking up von Stolberg's tail, the longer the margin of time the German could seize, the safer he would be. Depth charges took three times as long to sink to four hundred feet as to two hundred. Unlike an object falling through the air, they fell more slowly as the depth increased, because the water was denser at the lower level.

In diving to one hundred and fifty meters he had gone as deep as he cared to go in his present boat, and even at that depth she creaked alarmingly. The new U-boats could go quite comfortably to two hundred meters—six hundred feet, and one had reported returning to the surface from as far down as seven hundred and fifty. *U-121* was an early boat of her class and had been chosen for her present mission because, being slightly larger than the more modern boats, she had greater endurance.

She was not now tilted at an angle. Schwachofer was taking her down gently on an even keel, because at the greater depth any momentary loss of control could not be so easily corrected.

The hydrophone voice pipe was calling:

"Destroyer astern—closing rapidly."

The propeller beat could now be heard in the boat. Von Stolberg listened carefully.

"What is your depth?"

"Just coming to one hundred and fifty, Herr Kapitan."

"Good." Then to Schrader the quartermaster: "Port twenty, steer two-one-oh."

Breathlessly the crew waited. The rumbling detonations sounded above them. One bulb went out. There was nothing more.

"He fires too shallow," von Stolberg said, and a cracked smile twisted his lips. Schwachofer noticed it. It was the Kapitan's first attempt at a smile that day. Perhaps it boded well. Perhaps they'd get out of this somehow. "Steady on course and depth," he reported.

Kunz noticed it too, and his young heart leapt. He had not enjoyed the bad shock. Not at all. Von Holem saw the smile too, and was relieved.

Schwachofer broke the silence. "Herr Kapitan, breakfast for the men?"

"Yes, of course. Have some food passed around, but nothing heated. We must conserve electricity."

Very soon tins of sardines and biscuits smeared with butter were being passed round the boat. The butter, real butter, at once assumed the taste of U-boat. So did the bread, which absorbed the taint most readily. Even the newly opened tins of sardines tasted of diesel oil, mold, and sweat. The atmosphere was already becoming foul by ordinary standards, and they had only been submerged for three hours. The smell was part of their arduous duty—some-

95

thing all accepted and must learn to overcome. The boat sweated terribly. Clothes would not dry properly, and leather garments mildewed green over night and added to the unmistakable smell of U-boat.

Von Stolberg, stuffing a sardine into his mouth, called down the voice pipe to the hydrophone cabinet. "Well?"

"Enemy transmissions on our beam, drawing aft. I think he's going astern of us again, Herr Kapitan. His engines are turning very slowly."

The Kapitan finished his breakfast and asked again: "Well?"

"Still astern of us, Herr Kapitan. He's just sitting on our tail at the same course and speed."

"Zum Teufel," the Kapitan murmured. What was the mad Britisher up to now? To trail him as a detective trails a criminal? To creep continuously behind him? It was not war, it was annihilation! The books said that the British always attacked, and went on attacking wildly, until their ammunition was exhausted—then they went away. Suppose the destroyer should stay there all day? And all night too? The U-boat would have to be brought to the surface about six o'clock tomorrow, her endurance exhausted, and then the swine would get him without the expenditure of one single depth charge more.

And the *Cecilie?* Was the destroyer going to come all the way with him to his rendezvous? Had she already told the British Admiralty that there was a U-boat in the area? What did the naval information say on that score? It said that the British always made a sighting report immediately they were in contact with a German aircraft or a U-boat, but that thereafter they kept silence unless they achieved a victory. Only then did they break wireless silence again. He must assume that the British Captain would have reported at once. That was when? Eight o'clock on the previous night. Mad this particular pest might be, but he would hardly be so crazy as to disregard the rules of authority. Trying to put himself in the position of his opponent, he could not bring himself to believe that the sighting report had not been made at least twelve hours before. The message would have contained a geographical position, and that position would have been at least one hundred and fifty miles away to the northeast, and would be over two hundred miles from the position of his rendezvous with the *Cecilie*. He thought that there could be no possible chance that the report would bring a hornets' nest about the ears of the ship that he was going to meet.

If he could not sink the destroyer himself, and he had by no means given up hope that he would yet be successful, he was sure that the *Cecilie* would be only too pleased to do so when she arrived. At that late hour any further report the destroyer could make would be too late to prevent the transfer to him of the valuable documents. It was true that such a report might put the *Cecilie* herself in some jeopardy. But unless superior enemy surface forces were very near at hand, her chances of a safe return to the Fatherland were not likely to be greatly diminished. The sea was so vast, and her own disguise would be so good.

Looking at his watch, he saw that it was half-past ten. He went again to the hydrophone cabinet.

"Braun, where is she now?"

"Just the same, Herr Kapitan. She is coming slowly along behind us."

"I am going to see if he is asleep or not. It is just possible that he behaves so because a part of his machine is broken, and he waits like this while his men mend it. I am going to turn ninety degrees to port. You will tell me exactly what happens. I want to know if he follows me or not—you understand?"

"I understand, Herr Kapitan."

Von Stolberg went back to the control room.

"Alter course to one-two-oh degrees."

Feeling his boat begin to turn, he wondered whether the destroyer would follow him around. He prayed that she might go on. Not only because if she did so he might slip away from her but so that she would not be hanging on his tail any longer. It was a sensation that he particularly disliked. His analogy between detective and criminal had been an apt one. He felt just as a fugitive from justice might feel; and he was quite unable to appreciate the irony of the situation.

He tried to appear nonchalant, but so great was the effort that he was forced to give it up and go back to the hydrophone cabinet. He hated himself for thus giving way to weakness, and laid this as a further charge against the accursed Britisher.

There was a repeater from the gyrocompass on the bulkhead above the complicated instruments. Looking at it, he saw that his boat was steadied on her new course.

"Well, Braun?"

"Nothing further to report, Herr Kapitan."

"You mean that he is still there?"

"Ja, Herr Kapitan, as before."

98

Von Stolberg felt that the hair on the back of his head was rising. He smoothed his hand over his close-cropped head and retraced his steps to the control room.

"Alter back to course two-one-oh."

It was possible that another turn might yet catch his tracker unawares. Those in the destroyer would be so pleased with their first success that they might miss the second turn.

But it was to no purpose. The destroyer followed him around as confidently as before. There was evidently nothing the matter with her instruments, and this unwelcome knowledge was the only gain to set against the waste of a further fifteen minutes.

7

THE *Hecate,* barely making steerageway through the glittering tropical waves, followed the enemy below. It was a strange *cortège.*

Lulled by the gentle motion, the sailors basked in the sun—at any rate those who were not tending to the essential chores of food and keeping the ship clean. Flying fish, when disturbed, broke from the blue waters. They traveled airborne a short distance and then fell back skittering into the water. A few small clouds chased themselves in a circle around the horizon. Above the ship the sky was clear blue.

"What a wonderful day for it." The Doctor joined the Captain on the bridge.

"You've always been screaming for an action ever since you joined—now you've got it. What do you think of it?"

"All right as far as it goes. I must say that I'd expected more excitement—more *élan.*"

"Actions vary as much as men. We've a very peculiar one on our hands here. I need another ship to be really effective. But on the other hand I've got no convoy to worry about, and no fear of another U-boat trying to sink me while I deal with this one. He can't stay down for much longer than twenty-four hours. If I can keep on his tail, he'll have to come up, whether I blow him to the surface or just wait. Of course I admit it's a bit of a nervous strain on the asdic team and the plot. But we've got a dam' good crowd."

"I'd like to see him blown up, please."

"What bloodthirsty fellows you medical men are— I'd much rather catch 'em alive-oh."

"Just so that you can ask him what he's doing?"

"That for one reason anyway. He's obviously going somewhere. That somewhere is important to the German war effort or he wouldn't be here. My job is to jam it sooner or later, and I'd just as soon have it later because we might be able to learn what it is he's after. We have already accompanied him for one hundred and fifty miles."

"Good God! A far as that?"

"It's that far since I took your unguarded queen."

"Don't remind me."

"Want your revenge?"

"What—now?"

"I don't see why not. It's probably a little against the usual custom of the Navy for the Captain to play chess while his men are at action stations, but it's hardly against the tradition. Go and get the board. It will help to prevent me from becoming a giggling lunatic, which I might well do if I have to sit on this joker's tail for twenty-four hours."

So the Captain and the Doctor sat down on the platform round the standard compass, and the chessmen were set out.

"My turn for white," the Captain said.

"I hate playing black against you, sir. You're hard enough to beat anyway, without giving you the advantage of a start."

"Stand by for action then," the Captain answered, moving his queen's pawn two squares forward.

The bell from the asdic hut buzzed. The Captain was at the voice pipe in one bound. "Forebridge."

"Submarine altering course, sir. Bearing red one-oh. Range decreasing."

"Port twenty," the Captain called to the wheel-house.

"Target still drawing left, sir."

"Who is it on the set?"

"Macnally, sir," and a new voice: "Thomson speaking, sir. I'm here and Mr. Hopkins is just coming."

"Well done. I'm turning to port after him. The bearing should steady soon."

"Still drawing left, sir. Red four-oh."

The submarine, half a mile ahead and turning, was forty-five degrees on the bow. As the destroyer came around after her, the target would draw ahead once more.

"Bearing now?" the Captain asked.

"Bearing steadying," Hopkins' voice replied. A pause, and then: "Bearing drawing right. Red three-five."

The *Hecate* was swinging more quickly now. The

bearings came down steadily. Red two-oh. Red one-five. Fine on the port bow.

" 'Midships," the Captain ordered, "how's her head, Number One?"

"One-two-five, sir." The First Lieutenant had glanced at the standard compass.

"He's done a ninety-degree turn to port. Steer one-two-oh."

"Aye aye, sir."

"I bet he won't stay long on this course. It's just a wiggle to see if he can shake us off. He'll be turning back as soon as he finds out we're still behind him."

"Forebridge," from the asdic.

"Forebridge," replying.

"Submarine altering course—drawing right."

"Starboard twenty," the Captain said.

Dutifully the *Hecate* turned back to two-one-oh following the submarine. The Captain reseated himself before the board. "Your move, Doctor."

The sun still shone and the *Hecate* ambled after her prey.

"What beats me is how they get the men to do it."

"Do what?" the Captain asked.

"Go and sit there in that coffin ahead."

"This might be the coffin," the Captain said. "They sink a lot of ships—escorts too."

"What I've never understood is the ethics of the submarine game. If you ask any layman, he'll tell you that the Germans have U-boats that are utterly loathsome but that the British go to sea in submarines which are somehow quite another thing."

103

"Good God! You're not falling for that old one are you?"

"What do you mean, sir, falling for it? Isn't it true?"

"Of course it's not. Have you never been in touch with a submariner's mess in operational waters? No, I don't suppose you have. If you had, you would know the answer. There are very, very few areas where a 'sink-at-sight' policy is allowed. The Admiralty is most terribly strict about it too. Often our chaps have to risk their lives and their ships when they surface to tell the crews to get into the boats, knowing that the wretched target will make an enemy report and that in a few hours the area will be most unhealthy. There *are* just a few sink-at-sight areas, but the enemy is informed of those, and if he sends ships into them— why then it's his own funeral if he gets them sunk. But believe me, unrestricted submarine warfare has never been part of British naval practice—except of course against enemy warships. That's quite a different matter. Your move, Doctor."

So the forenoon wore on.

At half-past eleven the *Hecate* drew her sword again. The Captain explained his plan to the team. "I'm going to steam over her to get some idea of depth. Probably he'll think I'm attacking and he'll turn to port or starboard. When I come round again I will attack, but because I fancy he's wedded to this course of two-one-oh I think he'll turn back to it. So I'll keep that side of him. We might get him that way, because he'll turn into the pattern. Now get to your stations."

As a plan it had every chance of success. Shivering

in every fiber of her slim body, the *Hecate's* speed increased. One run over the target provided an estimated depth of four hundred feet, and the U-boat turned to starboard. The *Hecate,* attacking up her enemy's stern, kept, as near as could be judged, seventy-five yards on her port bow. The charges were fired and the Captain went to the view plot.

"Contact astern, green one-six-oh. Range four hundred—double echoes," announced the asdic.

The bearing and range at once suggested to the Captain that his enemy had double-bluffed him. Instead of turning to port and directly back to his course, he had turned a complete circle to starboard, and would have been far away from the bursting charges. The normal procedure would have been for the *Hecate* to turn to starboard too, but if he turned the other way and went straight for the target there was a possibility of having a beam-on shot at the U-boat instead of this wretched creeping-up-the-tail business. The double echoes almost certainly suggested that one was the U-boat and the other her wake.

"Port thirty."

He explained the supposition to the navigator on the plot.

The *Hecate* swung round. The target was on the port bow, the bearing steady. Her Captain had not meant to fire another pattern so soon. He had only sixty charges left and in less than five minutes there would be only fifty. At the last moment he had the sensation that the U-boat, surprised, was trying to take some violent evasive action—but he could not be certain. She was still there after the attack. Still on her course of two-one-oh.

The plot when consulted suggested that the firing of the charges had been a little late, and that with a crossing target they had passed too far ahead of the enemy. But it did suggest that the charges from the port thrower could have hit the enemy full on the nose.

Dutifully the *Hecate* took station astern of her quarry once more.

8

THE BRITISH Captain was quite right. Von Stolberg had tried a double bluff. He had turned a full circle to starboard, and he had expected the *Hecate* to follow him round. He was so certain that this would be the course of events that Braun's anxious report: "Destroyer approaching from before the starboard beam," had taken him completely by surprise. A surprise that was so deep that his immediate reaction was to think Braun's report wrong, and even when this had been confirmed, to force himself to believe that another surface vessel had joined the hunt.

It is axiomatic that a Captain must believe his own deductions to be correct—otherwise he is bound to lose confidence in himself. What is an obvious virtue can, in certain circumstances, become a source of the greatest danger. The strain of war tends to fix intentions—if only because to reverse orders already given may lead to more confusion than new instructions can right.

107

Three precious minutes were lost while the German confirmed his worst fears. Had he acted at once, he would still have had time to have swung his ship away from the attacker. The three lost minutes could never be regained. The only remaining course was for him to turn toward the enemy, in the expectation that the destroyer would have anticipated him turning away, and she would then fire late rather than early. "Starboard thirty," he ordered.

"Starboard thirty," Schwachofer replied.

A minute later the charges began to explode. This time they were correctly set for depth—that much was apparent. White-faced, with beads of perspiration on his forehead, the German waited. Then there was a shattering explosion that produced just the same sensation that would have been expected if the boat had run her nose into a rock. As an experience it was awful enough, although not to be compared with that endured earlier in the morning. Those of her crew that were standing up were flung forward, clutching desperately at anything that they could. Although the main fuses remained intact, all the lights in the forepart of the ship were broken once again. It was obvious to all aboard that the charge had exploded ahead; and that since, by her shape, the boat was best able to stand a shock from that direction, she had suffered far less than if the explosion had been on the beam or beneath her. What her crew could not know was that the shock had damaged the delicate mechanism in at least two of the torpedoes in her forward tubes. And although the *Hecate* had not, in this attack, done any material damage to her enemy's hull, she had in fact saved herself.

Von Stolberg was coldly furious, and basically his anger was directed at himself. Success in naval, as in any, warfare was often attributable to the mistakes of the other side. He had made a mistake, and the effect had nearly been disastrous. It was not even a big mistake. No one could have found fault with his decisions. It was only in the procedure. The three lost minutes had proved to be of paramount importance. The cold rage that possessed him made him determine to sink his adversary. But to do that he must come up from the depths. The destroyer, Braun informed him, had taken station astern once more. He supposed that she was enjoying an interval for lunch. It was just the sort of crazy action that he would expect from this particular ship. Already he was forming a very clear mental picture of the character of his foe. She was efficient certainly, sometimes brilliantly so, as when she had regained contact after losing it early in the morning; but at the same time he had a feeling that she could be tricked by cunning. She was no plodder, but an improviser. Surely Germanic thoroughness should be able to defeat the British originality?

He bent over the attack table and called to Schwachofer to help him.

"The Britisher must be sunk. Let us consider how we may achieve that. We will assume that we have gone up to twenty meters from where we can fire our torpedoes. Then what happens? The destroyer will decide to attack. It will first pass over us without dropping charges as it did just now, probably to ascertain our depth. We will turn, shall we say, to starboard. So long as we decide beforehand which way—it is no matter. The destroyer will run on like this——"

The Kapitan took a pencil from the tray and sketched the turn on the paper. "You see he will turn the same way as we turn, and at a range of about one thousand meters. Very well. We will fire a spread of four angled torpedoes. Let us work it out, Schwachofer. There, you see. One hundred, ninety, eighty, and seventy degrees angling. He will be beam-on to us, and one torpedo at least is bound to hit. With luck two torpedoes."

"But first we must come to twenty meters."

"I think the British Captain has his lunch now. I know it will not be easy to blow the tanks without making so much noise that the destroyer will hear. But I do not ask you to carry out this delicate maneuver in twenty minutes. I give you one whole hour —perhaps more."

"I will do my best, Herr Kapitan."

"Good. Then let us go up. In any case, if it is reported to the destroyer's Captain that we are blowing tanks, they will think that we come up because we can not stay down—and they will not attack us then. The poor fools are too softhearted. They will wait in the hope of rescuing survivors. But they will be the survivors—not us. We shall not attempt to pick them up —except perhaps just one as a keepsake."

Though Schwachofer did not relish being made the confidant of the Kapitan's thoughts, the plan was a good one. They might indeed be successful in sinking the enemy ship. She was a warship and therefore liable to be sunk by an enemy. Also it was obviously impossible to stow all her crew in *U-121*. The facts did not make him feel physically ill—it was the mentality of the man who recited them. How could a real sailor such as he delight in the destruction of ships and sailors' lives?

These thoughts did not in any way affect his efficiency as an officer of *U-121*. "Shall I start blowing now, Herr Kapitan?" he asked.

"Yes—very gently."

"Jawohl, Herr Kapitan."

"Müller," the Kapitan called. "When we reach twenty meters prepare the four forward tubes for firing."

"How long shall I have, Herr Kapitan?"

"How the devil should I know? When the accursed destroyer attacks, I shall require them immediately." Müller scuttled forward. The Kapitan was in a bad temper and he was thankful to be out of the way.

In the forward torpedo room Müller found the crew lying about. They sat up when he came in—all except one, who still lay on his back. In harbor they would have jumped to attention, but in a submerged boat the use of energy was cut to a minimum in order to conserve the very limited amount of air: a man working used up twice as much air as one who was not. Even so, the reclining member of the crew irritated the recently berated petty officer. "Sit up, damn you," he said, swinging a foot sharply to the man's buttocks.

Slowly, stealthily, *U-121* rose from the depths. In an hour and a quarter she was at twenty meters, and from that depth she could fire her torpedoes. It was then fifteen minutes past one, but she had to wait for a further two and a quarter hours before her intended prey made any move.

The atmosphere in the boat by that time was becoming foul. Breathing was nauseating, for all the air in the boat had already been through some man's lungs —and they had only been submerged for some nine hours. Later they would be permitted to use a special breathing apparatus like a gas mask that would guard against the deadly carbon-monoxide fumes. It would be but a poor palliative, for the rubber mouthpiece tasted horrible. Already men were sneaking to their lockers for a tablet of pervitin or caffein to stave off the awful soporific effect that the bad air had on their systems.

At last Braun made the long-awaited report.

"Enemy speed increasing."

They could hear her now—moving up—very close above their heads at this lesser depth. The roar of the powerful propellers reached a climax.

"Starboard thirty," von Stolberg ordered. "Course three-oh-oh. Stand by tubes one to four. Oberleutnant von Holem, take charge of the attack table. Target red nine-oh. Speed one-five knots. Range one thousand meters. Torpedo speed forty knots. Depth five meters."

"Attack table lined up," von Holem replied, making the switch that connected the table to the gyrocompass.

"Follow attack table," he gave the order to the forward torpedo room. The constantly changing firing settings were then being transmitted automatically to the torpedoes and set on their firing mechanisms. The torpedoes would fan out so that one at least was sure of a hit.

Von Holem was watching the Kapitan, who in turn was watching the gyrocompass. The Kapitan nodded. The boat lurched.

112

"Torpedo running," Braun announced.

The boat lurched again.

"Torpedo running," from Braun.

A third lurch.

Silence.

Every man in the control room waited.

"Torpedo not running," Braun said.

The Kapitan swore under his breath and the men swore aloud. The boat lurched again as the fourth torpedo left the tube.

"Torpedo running" and then in an excited cry: "Herr Kapitan, Herr Kapitan!"

"Yes, what is it?"

"I'm getting torpedo hydrophone effect on the starboard beam. Bearing growing aft."

"Himmel! A rogue torpedo." To Schwachofer: "Emergency dive to one hundred meters. One of our torpedoes is circling."

The *Hecate's* last attack had indeed saved her from disaster. The damaged gyro of the second torpedo had set it circling—more of a danger to the U-boat that had fired it than ever it would be to the destroyer. A fractured pipe in the engine of the third torpedo had prevented its starting at all. The deadly weapon was sinking harmlessly into the depths below. Only numbers one and four were running correctly. But as they fanned out on their diverging courses, there was space between their tracks into which a destroyer might turn —if she sighted them in time.

Mopping the sweat from their foreheads, the men of *U-121* took her back into the depths.

9

THE SUN, that had been so welcome in the freshness of morning, now beat down mercilessly on the *Hecate's* unprotected bridge. Intending to make it offer the greatest possible protection to the men who must man it in action, the designers had never assumed that a destroyer would conduct her warfare at slow speed under a tropical sun. The bridge was deep—shoulder-high to a medium-sized man; and above the metal sides were armored glass windshields a foot in height. Within its circumference there was only one spot of shade—at the front of the bridge, and projecting forward over the wheelhouse below, there was a narrow charthouse. The air within this space was unbearably hot, for the sides of the hut were so sun-heated that the hand could not be rested upon them. However, the rays could not strike directly into this retreat; and it was in there that the Captain sat on the deck, using a duffle coat as a cushion.

It was, as the Captain had suspected, going to prove a long and weary battle, and he had no qualms in seeking as much physical comfort as he could. For he was well aware that the rapid functioning of his own brain was as much a part of his ship's armament as the depth charges themselves.

He had no means of knowing how near his attacks had been to his opponent. As far as he could be certain, they had achieved no result at all; and the last time, when the U-boat had turned a complete circle and had given him an opportunity to attack across her course, he had expended one more of his meager supply of patterns. He had now only fifty depth charges left. He looked at his watch. Three o'clock. In nine hours he had used half his available ammunition, and it was quite possible that the underwater battle would go on until the following dawn.

Feeling the need of air in the heat of the little charthouse, he yawned and wished for the cool of evening. The steady ping of the asdic, with its satisfactory pong, told that the target was still held, but it had an effect that was immensely soporific. His head felt heavy and his eyes closed, fluttered, and closed again. It was pleasant to shut his eyes and think. To imagine himself back in an English garden, with sunlight filtering through the leaves of the trees. His wife would be there, and the children, two dogs, a cat, and the tame rabbit in the wire pen that was labeled "Daisy's End." Possibly there would be many other little Daisies by now. It had seemed an event that might be expected at any moment when he had last been on leave. On the other hand it could possibly be the result of overeating. Daisy was an unpredictable brute, and as

115

likely to lash out at grownups as to allow herself to be mauled by children.

It was funny what peculiar desires came to one in far-off places. He would like to hear the crisp sound of a ball on a bat, although he was no cricketer and never had been. But here, miles at sea, and in contact with the enemy, he wanted the sounds that had been bound up with his own youth. He wondered if the Herr Kapitan down below had ever played cricket. He thought not. There was something about the British games that passed other nations by—even when they tried to play them. Would Junkers be Junkers if their forefathers had been able to play cricket on the village green with their tenantry? Probably not.

He imagined that the Germans below—the Germans in the pong that came back from the asdic—were held there by an iron and inhumane discipline. Terribly efficient they might be, but could a ship, a city, or a country be run without compassion? It had looked at one time as if Hitler and his minions could do so. But now the thing seemed to be breaking up. Cracks were appearing in the façade—but not yet in the U-boat arm, where discipline was strongest if only because the common danger was greatest.

"Captain, sir. Captain, sir." It was his First Lieutenant's voice.

"Yes, Number One?"

"Five minutes to fifteen-thirty, sir."

"Thank you." He rose slowly from his hard couch and went out into the sun.

"Everything just the same?"

"Just the same, sir."

"Your turn to have a rest after this attack—I'll take her in the 'dogs.' Don't be ashamed of dropping off. This isn't ordinary routine."

"Thank you, sir."

"God, it's hot! Tell the depth-charge parties to stand by, and warn the asdic and the engine room." He turned to look at the apparently empty sea ahead. The *Hecate's* flaring bow moved slowly over the waves. It rose and fell purposefully. The gun crew below him were whistling a tune in unison. It was, he noticed, really rather well done. Many of them had been closed up at the gun, except for short dashes to the "heads," since six in the morning.

"Coxswain at the wheel, sir." His Coxswain's voice sounded metallic, reaching him through the voice pipe.

"Thank you, Coxswain."

The *Hecate,* gathering speed, crept up on her quarry. Her Captain had expected to find the U-boat still deep. He was surprised to find it so near the surface. "Artful blighter," he remarked when it was plain that the enemy had turned to starboard as he had swept over her. Very well, he'd play the same game. Turn to starboard too. It would force the German to go full circle again and he might, by bluff, be able to get across him once more. He was shallow too, and that gave less chance of error in the depth-charge settings. They might even blow her to the surface, and he'd see her again. He'd like to see her. After more than nine hours of knowing her only as an echo, he needed confirmation that the whole thing was not a mare's-nest. A glimpse of a gray hull among the ex-

117

ploding depth charges would be a rewarding sight.

The *Hecate* was turning now, parallel to the U-boat's new course.

"High-speed hydrophone effect," Hopkins' voice reached him. The officer might just as well have said torpedoes. After their experience of the morning there was no forgetting the sound that was once more coming from the bridge loud-speaker. A clattering roar that grew louder each second.

So that was what the fellow was doing at a shallow depth—firing angled torpedoes by instruments! There was only one course open: turn bows toward the U-boat in order to make the target as small as possible.

"Starboard thirty. Half-astern starboard engine. Full ahead, port."

But with a running time of only a fraction over a minute, the torpedoes would probably arrive before his ship had begun to answer his command.

The First Lieutenant had jumped onto the platform of the starboard signal lamp. The Captain had leapt to the platform on the opposite side—only the second officer of the watch was left on the deserted compass platform. The ship vibrated wildly as her starboard engine began to run astern and her port one full ahead. Her bows were swinging rapidly over the sea, hauled around by thirty thousand horsepower.

"Torpedo passing clear on the starboard bow," the first Lieutenant's shout reached the Captain's ears. A moment later he saw the second as it appeared across the bows going away to port. The long white trail of its wake undulated over the waves. Fascinated, he watched it disappear into the blue.

Between the two that they had seen, there should have been two more—and they would have torn out the vitals of his ship. Fortunately it was these two that were missing.

"Half-ahead both—one-five-oh revolutions. Asdic hut, range and bearing of target please."

The *Hecate* swept into attack once more, but her charges, set to kill a U-boat at torpedo-firing depth, did little more than annoy the boat that was already plunging downward.

"So he tried to kipper us?" It was the Doctor speaking.

"He did indeed," the Captain answered. "And we were very lucky to get away with it. The Herr is a very determined man, and besides having us on his tail, I'm pretty sure that he's got a load of mischief on his mind."

"How long will it take him to reload? I suppose he does carry spares?"

"Oh yes, he carries spares all right—but it's not quite as easy as that. They need a good hour and a half to do it in, and they must have absolute quiet while they are working. Imagine trying to handle over a ton of slippery metal in a U-boat. No fun at all. I very much doubt if he'll reload while we are still in contact. Of course he may have two more—but I doubt it. Those torpedoes were angled so far apart that they'd have missed even if we had not begun to turn. My bet is that he fired his four bow tubes and that the two center ones failed to run because of a mechanical breakdown due to the hammering that we've given him."

"What do you make of his character, sir?"

"You think the same way as I do. I've already invested him with a character—arrogant, a bigot, and a strict disciplinarian with no trace of humanity—a real Junker. I can almost imagine his face. He'll yield obedience to the letter of his superior's law as determinedly as he'll extract it from those junior to him. He's been told to carry out an operation, and he's damn well going to do it unless the *Hecate* can stop him. He's a plodder but dangerous just because he will never give up. He's not brilliant. He had a chance this morning to sneak off, but he didn't take it. A man less hidebound would have done so, and trusted to good fortune to turn the tide in his favor again once he was rid of us. Possibly the discipline has been so severely beaten in to him that he feared that a breakaway to the southeast this morning would appear to the U-Boat Command as a lack of decision and determination on his part. In my opinion he's hagridden by the discipline of his own thought."

"If you're right it makes him quite a case."

"Well, aren't they all? I bet you, Doc, that if Germany were to crack tomorrow and we were to walk in, we wouldn't find one damn Nazi in the whole of Germany. Overnight they'd all have changed to the 'good kind.' You know how we say that there are good and bad ones. I don't believe it. They're all the same at heart. Oh, I suppose that's not quite fair—there may be the odd one that's presentable. But they're not fixed characters. They're malleable, and can be squeezed by Hitlers and Kaisers into any chosen mold."

"When are you going to attack again, sir?"

"Unless anything fresh happens, at seven-thirty and

120

eleven-thirty tonight, and at three-thirty and dawn tomorrow. I've only four patterns left. I had intended
to stir him up in the first dog at five-thirty, but I'll
have to drop that one from the list. I spent two patterns instead of one at noon today."

"He'll begin to hate you."

"I expect he does that already."

10

VON STOLBERG did indeed hate the Captain of the destroyer that was persecuting him. Particularly because he had just noticed that both the attack at midday and the last one had been made half an hour before the watch would normally have been changed.

The thought that the Britisher was reducing his attacks to occur at regular intervals drove the German frantic. It made the time that would otherwise have appeared to be a respite into nothing but an agonizingly long and drawn-out prelude to the next attack. It was an insult to the power of his own craft.

Did this give him time to reload? If the hypothesis was correct, then he would have the necessary quiet period. But he could not be certain. He could never be quite certain. What ill fate had put this bloody man on his trail? Driven deep, the sting of his torpedoes drawn, the air getting fouler every hour, and his batteries running low, von Stolberg knew himself to be in his tightest corner yet.

Up above them the sun would be settling in the west. In an hour it would be dark. Perhaps then the destroyer would lose contact—for her men must be as weary as his own. The British Captain and his team of trained ratings would have been at their instruments for over twelve hours. The human frame was not indestructible—even the Germanic frame was not—so it would more readily crack in an inferior race. When the destroyer next attacked at seven-thirty—"Blöder Kerl," the Kapitan said to himself. "I fall into the very trap that he has set for me."

When next the destroyer attacked he would use his last two remaining *pillenwerfer* and see if they could slip away before the tired men in the destroyer were aware of his escape.

Schwachofer moved from the corner, where he had been resting tired legs by leaning against the bulkhead.

"Herr Kapitan, shall I warn Braun?"

"Of what?" Von Stolberg spun round.

Schwachofer looked down at the watch on his wrist.

"That the enemy may attack, Herr Kapitan."

The knowledge that others had detected a pattern to the action of his enemy only added fire to his own anger. The whole boat would have the jitters if he were not careful.

He drew himself up to his full slim height and looked his burly junior coldly in the eye. "I see no reason to suspect any particular time of attack. Such a supposition would be highly dangerous and, Herr Oberleutnant, very bad for morale."

"Herr Kapitan," the voice pipe from the hydrophone cabinet called. "The destroyer is increasing speed." Braun sounded desperately weary.

"Müller, stand by *pillenwerfer.*"

Schwachofer turned away. In looking into those cold blue eyes he had detected both the anger and the lie. He smiled a little ruefully to himself. But his face was toward the big depth-recording dial. None but he knew about the smile, and there was no glass in which it could be reflected.

The *U-121* turned to port as the destroyer passed above her. And to port again as she ran in a second time.

"Release two *pillenwerfer.*"

They were gone—his last attempt to muddle and defeat the enemy. The two bubbling cones hung in his wake.

Braun was calling from the hydrophone room.

"Destroyer reducing speed, Herr Kapitan."

Were they going to creep away? The whisper of the asdic lash on the hull seemed less. But that could be just their own imagining—or possibly the blanketing effect of their own *pillenwerfer.*

Swish—swish—the lash never left them. It grew stronger again as the destroyer followed them through the disturbed water—followed them into the clear sea beyond.

There was not a man in the boat whose face was not set and grim.

"Destroyer attacking," Braun announced.

11

ALL THROUGH the night the *Hecate* hung on
to her adversary. Cups of steaming cocoa
were carried around to her men, who were lying down,
huddled in duffle coats or oilskins, alongside the weap-
ons they served. Three times during the night they had
attacked. Now only one last pattern of depth charges
remained.

The first hint of dawn showed in the east. Stiffly her
Captain stirred from the trancelike state in which he
had been leaning against the corner of the bridge.

"Number One—of your charity—cocoa for all on
the bridge. As soon as it's fully light, we'll give him
our last pattern. He's a real desperate character, this
one, but he's only got the standard batteries and a
limited amount of air. I don't think he can stand much
more than another hour or two, and then the guns
can deal with him."

The navigator climbed the ladder to the bridge carrying his sextant.

"Morning stars?" the Captain asked.

"Yes, sir."

"I wonder if we ought to push out another signal?" The Captain was thinking aloud. "It may help to let people know what's happening to us. We're almost a hundred miles from our position at dawn yesterday, and two hundred and forty from where we picked up our German bear-leader."

Yeoman Willis appeared as if by magic at the Captain's elbow. He had a nose for a signal that was as sensitive as that of any retriever for a fallen bird.

"You wish to make a signal, sir?"

In spite of the tiredness that almost overwhelmed him, the Captain laughed. "Willis, I was considering the possibility—only considering. Don't look so disappointed. I probably shall do so. In fact I think I will. Make to Admiralty, repeated C-in-C, South Atlantic: *Still in contact. Enemy course unaltered. Depth charges expended,*" and get the position from the navigator."

"Aye aye, sir."

The Captain watched navigator and yeoman go down the ladder—the one to the charthouse on the deck below, and the other to the wireless office. He called after the navigator: "Pilot, let me know as soon as you've got a position—I'll want you on the plot when I attack." He turned to receive the hot cocoa from the bosun's mate.

"Gosh—this is good." He stood beside his First Lieutenant. "Feeling tired, Number One?"

"Not so bad as I might be, sir." The officer was holding his chilled hands around his warm cup.

"Neither am I. I was worst off about three hours

ago. Now I seem to have got my second wind. Just a tight feeling round my head as if my cap was too small, and a terrific heat under my eyelids when I shut them."

"How much longer will it go on, sir?"

"No one can tell. He may not even fight his gun, although I never see why so many of them don't. But then again, there are generally two or more escorts. I've always thought that if I were a German U-boat commander I'd try and do something with my cannon. After all, he's a terribly small target for us. Only about three hundred square feet and very little of that area is vulnerable. Our semi-armor-piercing shells will just bounce off it. We'd spoil its looks but we wouldn't damage its pressure hull. They've got a target that is ten times as big to aim at, and the whole area is to some extent vulnerable—a destroyer is so packed with stuff that she can hardly take any damage without losing some important part of her fighting efficiency."

"Forebridge." The voice came from the plot.

"Yes, Pilot?" the Captain answered.

"Ready now, sir."

"What was the position?"

"Five north, thirty-two west."

"Exactly?"

"As near as dammit, sir."

"Sounds just the sort of staff office choice for a rendezvous—I wonder if we have arrived. Dear, oh dear, the Herr Hun will be cross if we've tagged along to his trysting place. Let's attack him now. The sun's nearly up. He's been deep the last three times. I'm not going to carry out a dummy run this time. I'm just

127

going straight in to attack with four hundred and fifty feet on the charges. We may catch him napping, particularly as we are out of the routine that we've been training him to expect. We attacked only three hours ago. He won't be expecting us for another hour. Tally ho, chaps. Range and bearing, Mr. Hopkins, please?"

NIGHT in *U-121* had appeared interminable, for each of the destroyer's attacks had seemed like gigantic minute guns that spoke of doom. At midnight the order had been given for her crew to put on their anticarbon-monoxide masks, but the discomfort of wearing these for such a long period had proved almost as trying to their tempers as the deadly gas would have been to their bodies. Caffein and pervitin tablets had kept her crew awake, but constant recourse to such stimulants was having a deplorable effect on their nerves.

Von Stolberg, by exercise of his own fierce self-control, still held his fraying crew together. At three o'clock had occurred an incident that had threatened to shake morale badly.

Müller had staggered into the control room. "Herr Kapitan! It is young Edelmann—he has gone mad. It takes four men to hold him."

Von Stolberg turned his head to look at the petty

officer. Müller was shocked to see how his commanding officer appeared to have aged in the last few hours. The skin on either side of the rubber mouthpiece had a parchment-like quality. The unshaven beard made it appear like the face of one already dead.

Without answering directly the Kapitan crossed to the cabinet where the revolvers hung, and took one down. With only a partial turn of their heads the men in the control room watched him go. Their eyeballs gleamed in the dim light.

There was a sudden, small, unmistakable explosion, and burnt cordite joined the other smells in the boat. The white eyeballs glanced nervously at each other and then returned to their instruments.

The scuffling and muted swearing that had preceded the Kapitan's visit to the forward torpedo room had ceased.

"Achtung." Von Stolberg's voice cut the thick atmosphere. "That is the only medicine for those."

Even if the prompt treatment that the Kapitan had applied had resulted in a partial obliteration of thought, rather than a rebuttal of the weakness to which human beings are prone, the Kapitan's action had achieved its immediate object—that of preventing the further spread of hysteria.

Hour by hour little crosses had been penciled on the chart—each one nearer than the one before to the circle that denoted the rendezvous. The last, at six o'clock, had actually lain within the prescribed area. Whatever damage the destroyer had done, she had failed to prevent *U-121* from arriving at her rendezvous with six hours to spare.

"Achtung." Von Stolberg spoke again. "We have made our rendezvous. At noon the German cruiser *Cecilie* will join us and drive off the accursed destroyer. We have been successful in this. We shall be successful in the rest."

"Destroyer increasing speed." Braun made the report.

Perhaps Braun had been a little slow in detecting the increase in the beat of the destroyer's propellers. Perhaps the Kapitan had become so used to the feint run that the destroyer had made as a prelude to each of her six last attacks, that he delayed giving the order to turn. Perhaps it was just the exhaustion of her crew that made each piece of her thought process just that little bit slower. Whatever the cause, it is certain that she had barely started to turn when the destroyer passed overhead.

Von Stolberg realized at once that somewhere their corporate reflex had been slow, and he determined that next time, when the real attack came, they must do better.

The bursting of the first two charges astern of the U-boat took them all, and not least the Kapitan, entirely by surprise. He realized, perhaps better than any of them, the dangerous implication, and steeled both his body and brain against the impending shock. Four charges went off almost simultaneously; two on either side, above and below him. *U-121* was shaken as a rat by a terrier. In the toils of the enormous pressure waves, the boat was, at the same time, both pitched and rolled, first one way and then the other. Turning and twisting like a maddened fish, with her men again plunged into the near-darkness

131

of the emergency lighting, she would have hurtled to the bottom except that Schwachofer's skill prevented it. His art, and the fantastic luck that put her so exactly in the middle of the destroyer's pattern had, by a miracle, saved her hull from being utterly crushed.

Inside, the boat was a shambles. Fittings and pipes had been wrenched from their clips, and men lay in heaps where they had fallen. Only in the control room was there any semblance of order.

And then, to those orderly ones controlling her, there appeared in the semidarkness a thing that hopped and screamed. About the size of a small dog, it ran into a corner where it began to leap up and down, emitting a high-pitched wail.

Horrified, the clustered men stared at this apparition. Even von Stolberg felt his reason clamoring to be allowed to go. He clung to the periscope standard and looked at the thing.

"It's the gyrocompass, broken adrift." Schwachofer, the imperturbable, had guessed correctly. The gyro ring had been broken, and the gyro wheel, revolving at ten thousand revolutions, had gone careering through the boat.

Von Stolberg's eyes rose to meet those of his Executive Officer. He looked utterly dazed. "Surface," he gasped.

The engineer officer stumbled into the control room. He was coughing terribly. "Chlorine. Sea water leaking into number two battery."

Von Stolberg nodded. "We're going up. Be ready to start the diesels, Herr Engineer."

"You will never start them—never. I have withdrawn my men from the engine room and clipped the door shut—otherwise you would never reach the surface alive."

"It is as bad as that?"

"Jawohl, Herr Kapitan. Perhaps you may go for a little longer on the motors when you reach the surface. I do not know, for it is impossible to assess the damage. Already some of the cells are boiling."

Von Stolberg took this further blow with stoical calm. "We shall go back to Germany in the *Cecilie*." And to von Holem: "You are the gunnery officer. Have your gun crew ready to man the gun. I will fight him and sink him yet. He is a much bigger target than we. There is no reason why we should not have more prisoners for the *Cecilie*. You understand?"

"Jawohl, Herr Kapitan."

With the thought of seeing the light of day again, the morale of the men entombed in *U-121* was reviving. Anticipation was driving away the heaviness engendered by lack of sleep and the foul air. Some would undoubtedly be sick as soon as the clean air entered their lungs, but the gun crew would probably find their excitement able to overcome this common disability.

"Twenty meters," Schwachofer reported. The gun crew were already clustered at the foot of the ladder.

"Ten meters."

The gunlayer sprang up the iron rungs. His weight was thrown desperately on the wheel that retained the heavy hatch. The air pressure inside the boat was such that even if the hatch was opened a few feet below water, the air rushing out would prevent any material amount from entering.

The hatch, worked by its big spring, was raised. The dog that held it in place clicked into position. The gun crew poured out as fresh air rushed in.

"Open fire as soon as you can," the Kapitan had told von Holem. "Keep on firing, and try to give me the enemy's course so that I can keep the gun bearing."

BOOK THREE

Gun Battle

06.32, Zone Time, Thursday, 9 September, to 09.16,
Position 5° 00' N. 35° 00' W.

1

THE *Hecate's* wake lay curled in a great circle as she turned after her attack. On the outside of the circle the wash fanned out in broad flèches, but on the inside of the turn the waves met and jostled each other. The inquisitive sun was just peeping over the misty horizon as the ship's head turned to the eastward.

"Forebridge," the cry came from the asdic cabinet.

"Forebridge," the Captain answered.

"I think the U-boat's blowing her tanks, sir."

"Thank you, Mr. Hopkins, keep passing me the range and bearing." Then to the First Lieutenant: "Action stations, Number One. We must have a reception committee for him."

The sound of the alarms rattled through the ship. Her crew was almost instantly ready: to all intents and purposes she had had her hand on the hilt of the sword for twenty-four hours. She had only to draw it.

The asdic was speaking again.

"Bearing oh-three-oh. Very woolly echo. He's blowing, sir. Range nine hundred."

The bearing was broad on the starboard bow.

"Pass the bearings in 'relative bearings.' It will be easier for the guns."

"Aye aye, sir. Bearing green six-oh."

"Guns," the Captain spoke to the Gunnery Officer, "bring your guns to the ready. Submarine expected to surface about green six-oh."

"Aye aye, sir."

From the asdic: "Lost contact, sir."

The Yeoman appeared at the Captain's elbow. "Message passed, sir."

"Thank you, Yeoman."

Anxiously the men of the destroyer waited for the second sight of their quarry. Many had not seen her on the first occasion—and all expected an early termination to their vigil. It was to be supposed that she would surface, either so damaged that her men would at once begin to abandon ship or that the enemy would be induced to do so as the result of a short gun engagement. After four years of war the normal course of events was well known to all. Only the Captain himself had any idea of the exceptional circumstances in which the *Hecate* found herself; and even he was perhaps not yet fully alive to the difference between forcing a U-boat to the surface on the edge of a convoy where help was available, and doing the same in the middle of the ocean where he was all alone.

"U-boat surfacing," the cry went up from many throats.

"Permission to open fire, sir?" the Gunnery officer asked.

"Not yet, Guns. Let's see if they start abandoning ship. Yeoman, try and call them up with the light. I don't like firing on survivors. Make 'abandon' to them very slowly."

Willis sprang to the ten-inch signal lamp and began to flap the shutter, *clack—clack*. It was the only sound that the tense watchers on the bridge could hear.

"There they come, sir," the First Lieutenant cried excitedly.

Little figures could be seen pouring out of the conning tower. The U-boat was lying at an angle to the destroyer. The sun, now fully above the horizon, was dazzling the men in the surface ship, and the U-boat was moving slowly and steadily into the path of scintillating brilliance that the new day laid across the ocean.

"Dam' this sun," the Captain said.

"Target—a submarine. Bearing green five-five. All guns load, semi-armor-piercing shell." The Gunnery Officer was carrying out the routine drill.

"Someone's crawling aft," the First Lieutenant reported.

"*Clack—clack—clack—*" The signal projector started the word "*abandon.*" "*Clack-ety—clack-ety-ety——.*"

"B Gun ready."

"There's a hell of a lot of smoke from her." The Captain spoke. It was true. A vaporous cloud of yellow-green smoke was pouring out of the U-boat's stern.

139

"It's not diesel smoke either," the First Lieutenant answered.

"Looks as if she's on fire."

"X Gun ready."

"Salvoes. Range nine hundred," the Gunnery Officer said.

The sun, and the haze that billowed from the stern of their target, momentarily hid the U-boat from definite view.

A flash of orange in the haze, and before the destroyer's bow a plume of water rose where the shell had fallen close alongside.

"Fire," the Captain snapped.

"Shoot," the Gunnery Officer repeated into the curved mouthpiece that hung on his chest.

The *Hecate* shook to the dual crash as both the 4.7 guns fired within a split second of each other. Watching through steady binoculars, the group of officers waited to see the result of their first shots.

Only the Gunnery Officer, more single-minded in his own trade, saw the shells land just over the target. "Down one hundred, shoot," he ordered.

The other officers were leaning over the starboard side of the bridge looking down at their own vessel's side. The ship-shaking explosion that had sent them there had come from below them. Somewhere under the curve of the bow an enemy shell had hit. Clouds of acrid smoke were already eddying from the open ammunition hatch of B Gun.

The *Hecate's* guns fired again. In the Gunnery Officer's glasses he could see two columns of water on either side of the smoke that was the U-boat.

"Down one hundred. Rapid salvoes."

"Quick, Number One! Get down below and see what the damage is. I'll take her," the Captain said.

The First Lieutenant hurried from the bridge.

The guns fired again. A flash of orange that was not the U-boat's gun flared momentarily in the smoke.

"Nice shooting, Guns."

Again the guns fired. The *Hecate* at a steady speed was overhauling the U-boat.

"Down one hundred," the Gunnery Officer said.

The next moment an ear-splitting racket broke from the starboard side between the funnels where the twin-barrel Oerlikon could just be brought to bear. Essentially a close-range antiaircraft weapon, it was now firing at extreme range. The little red dots of its tracer bullets disappeared into the U-boat's unintentional smoke screen. The shells when they arrived could not in any way hurt the enemy, but they could kill men.

The *Hecate's* guns fired again. Then once more she shuddered as an enemy shell tore into her delicate superstructure. Entering above the level of the upper deck, it passed through the Bosun's locker and the Coxswain's cabin before it exploded against the strong trunk of B Gun.

The shock threw most of the gun crew to the deck. X Gun, aft, fired the salvo alone. B Gun reported "training jammed."

The First Lieutenant, his cap missing and his face bathed in sweat, climbed onto the bridge. "I've had to flood the for'rard magazine," he said. "The deck above was red hot."

"Christ!" the Captain answered, "half our ammunition gone."

"Couldn't be helped, sir. It was touch and go."

X Gun fired again.

"Much damage?"

"The blasted shell exploded in the naval stores. Coils of burning ropes. Small fires from the emergency lighting all over the place. Under control soon, sir."

"Any injured?"

"Three bad burn cases—no casualties."

"What about the second hit?"

"Blown the Coxswain's cabin to hell, sir. But no fires—everything was blown clean over the side."

X Gun fired again. The Oerlikons were firing in steady bursts.

The Captain stroked his unshaven chin.

"This damn fellow is even more of a problem up above than he was down below."

142

2

As the last of the gun crew tumbled up the conning-tower ladder, Otto Kritz, the engineer, approached the Kapitan, who stood staring up the open hatch at the circle of blue sky above.

"Permission to open the after escape hatch, Herr Kapitan. The fumes from the burning battery will make a good smoke screen."

"Excellent, Herr Engineer. At once."

The engineer climbed the ladder. For a moment his body blocked the hatch, then it was clear again. Von Stolberg turned to Schwachofer. "Run up the attack periscope so that I can see."

The periscope rose smoothly. The Kapitan trained the instrument. "Ha! We are up-sun of the enemy. Without the gyro we must have turned one hundred and eighty degrees as we surfaced. We are a very difficult target for him. Schwachofer, raise the small periscope and conn the quartermaster so that he steers to keep us between the Britisher and the sun. The fool is signaling. I suppose he hopes that we will surrender. The gun will be my answer to that."

At that moment the gun fired. The crash of its exploding charge shook the U-boat.

Kritz scrambled down the ladder. "The fumes are perfect, Herr Kapitan. Our own crew can see through them, but they will make it very hard for the destroyer."

The gun fired—and again.

"A hit," von Stolberg exclaimed delightedly.

"Where?" Schwachofer asked.

"Beneath the bridge somewhere. I saw the flash, and the smoke is pouring out of her forward superstructure. She is on fire. Perhaps she will blow up."

The U-boat shuddered with an explosion that was not made by its own gun.

The engineer ran up the ladder. He paused with his head and shoulders above the hatch.

"Only part of the after casing blown away. It is nothing, Herr Kapitan."

"Kritz, can I open the forward escape hatch?" von Stolberg asked.

"Jawohl, Herr Kapitan. There is only a very little sea, and that from astern. On this course it would be quite safe, and we can only go very slowly, for there is very little left in the battery."

"Then open it, Herr Engineer. If one of the gun crew is wounded it will be more easy to replace a casualty, and we shall be in better touch with von Holem. Ha!—another hit. The destroyer's forward gun has not fired. Oh, von Holem, von Holem, that is good shooting indeed. Kunz, tell Herr Oberleutnant von Holem that the destroyer's forward gun is out of action. Tell him to aim no longer at the bridge, but to aim between the funnels."

"Jawohl, Herr Kapitan."

Another shuddering crash came from just outside the hatch. Quick as a flash the engineer was up the ladder and a moment later down again.

"Well?" von Stolberg asked.

"The after end of the conning tower. There is much mess but no damage."

"What is the charge in number one battery?"

"Very low, Herr Kapitan. I do not think we can run the motors for much longer. Submerged, we would not make two knots. It is possible that on the surface we are making three. Barely steerageway."

Von Stolberg, who had removed his eyes from the periscope, trained the instrument again on the destroyer. It was obvious to him that, at the relative speed of the ships, the destroyer would soon overtake the U-boat. In any case he had not the speed necessary to allow him to keep up-sun of his antagonist. With one of her guns out of action, the destroyer's speed was now her only superiority. Every other advantage lay with the U-boat. He would, he thought, begin a slow turn to starboard, for the destroyer was coming up on his port side. By so doing he would give her the much larger outside circle to steam, while he would continually present the smallest possible target consistent with keeping his own gun bearing on the enemy.

The shelter of the conning tower had already saved the gun's crew once. Had the gun not been firing on an after bearing, the shell that had hit the after end of the tower would undoubtedly have wiped out the crew, even if it had not hit the gun itself.

"I am going to alter course," the Kapitan told Schwachofer, and to the quartermaster: "Starboard five."

Kunz returned to the control room. His eyes were elated and he spoke excitedly. "Von Holem has made two hits. I gave him your message. He says that he will sink the destroyer."

"Stand to attention when you address your commanding officer," von Stolberg snapped, taking his eyes for one moment from the periscope. "And do not forget that none of this would have been necessary if you had not been such a fool."

The gun fired again.

Greatly deflated, Kunz slunk back to his action position beside the now useless attack table. The *Kapitan* favored him with a baleful glance and so failed to observe the arrival of the shell that had just been fired.

3

THE CAPTAIN of the *Hecate* was now faced with a problem of some magnitude. His ship had already received serious damage, and his effective gunpower had been reduced by half, with the result that it was now no greater than that of his opponent. To withdraw out of the enemy's fire, while still remaining within the range of his more powerful gun, would be to so reduce the size of his target as to make the chances of a hit quite outside practical politics. To do this he would have to open the distance between the ships to somewhere between six and eight miles.

With his forward gun out of action, he could fire his after gun only if he kept his ship at quite a considerable angle to the enemy. On a course that would do this, the target that he offered to his adversary was large and highly vulnerable. To turn away, and so reduce the target he made for the German, while still keeping his after gun in action, was not only against his nature but would set his gunnery officer the very difficult problem of hitting while the range was continually opening. To achieve regular hits from such an unsteady platform as that provided by a small ship in the Atlantic, it was essential to keep the range as steady as possible.

The Yeoman was at his side. "Message for us, sir."

"What is it, Yeoman?"

"Signal from Admiralty, sir. Message reads: '*Acheron, Marabout, Mastiff diverted to your support oh-nine-oh-two yesterday. Anticipate arrive your position noon today. My oh-eight-five-eight of the eighteenth to Force M refers.*' "

Dragging his tired brain back from the immediate gunnery problem, the *Hecate's* Captain considered this information and all it implied. So the Admiralty, too, thought that something was afoot in this neglected quarter of the great ocean. The very make-up of the ships sent to join him was sufficient indication of that. One six-inch-gun cruiser, the *Acheron*, and two fleet destroyers—it was a force quite out of proportion to deal with one U-boat.

"I suppose we haven't decoded Admiralty's oh-eight-five-eight. Pity they didn't put our call signs in the heading. I expect Johnson will have read it—but of course among thousands of other signals it will take time to find and decode."

"I could ask for a repeat, sir, if you thought it justified breaking wireless silence."

"I don't, Willis. Certainly not that. In any case *Acheron* will have our present position relayed to her.

Tell Johnson to try and find Admiralty's oh-eight-five-eight of yesterday."

The conversation with his Yeoman had taken but a few minutes. But they were vital minutes indeed. Steering a steady course and moving much faster than the U-boat, the destroyer had almost drawn level with the enemy and, although she had opened the range, her whole silhouette was available as a target.

"Starboard ten," the Captain ordered as soon as he appreciated the position. He had, of course, no knowledge of conditions aboard the U-boat. It seemed that for some reason, probably connected with the smoke that was rising from her, she was temporarily unable to use her diesels. There was, however, absolutely no knowing whether she would be able to effect repairs, and if so, when these would be completed. At the moment it could be assumed that she was still running on the electric motors— but for how much longer she would have enough electricity in the batteries to keep these alive was the guess of anybody aboard the destroyer. Her unchar-acteristic fierceness, after being forced to the surface, could only be due to confidence—confidence that she could repair herself sufficiently if given time, or that, if she could hold out for long enough, help would come to her from some quarter about which the *Hecate's* Captain knew nothing.

The Captain noted that the bows of his ship were already swinging round to follow the turn that the U-boat had started. Now, thank heaven, the wretched boat was no longer up-sun of him. In fact, if the sub-marine were to continue its turn, the time would soon come when the relative positions would be reversed, and it would be the gunlayer of the submarine who would then have the sun in his eyes.

It was at this precise moment that the shell arrived that had been fired while the commanding officer of the U-boat had been distracted by his junior.

It plunged through the thin side plating at the after corner of number one boiler room, penetrated the bulkhead between that boiler room with its single boiler, and burst against the curved flank of the second boiler. The effects of this single hit were almost disastrous. The giant fans, whose high-pitched whirr was a constant feature of life in a destroyer, normally kept the boiler rooms under pressure while the torches were alight, in order to force the flame through the boilers and the hot gas up the funnel; and once the pressure was released through the torn side, the inevitable flashback occurred. For an instant before the automatic devices cut off the supply of oil, the boiler room was a searing furnace where tortured men shrieked in agony.

The position was bad in this boiler room, but it was even worse in the other. The bursting shell had destroyed at least a quarter of the tubes of number two boiler. From these tubes, and from the big main steampipe that was also damaged, there drained away every ounce of steam in the three boilers. In this room the crew died instantly.

From the bridge the particulars of the damage were not at once apparent. A huge cloud of steam rose in tortive waves from somewhere between the two funnels, carrying among its snow-white billows

150

the black oily smoke from the fire in the forward boiler room. The throb of the engines died.

"Ship's not answering her wheel, sir," the Coxswain reported.

The Captain knew he must think. No need to wait on a report to know that his ship had received a vital wound. The wind, which was light, was on his starboard quarter. As she lost her way through the water, the *Hecate* would turn ever more quickly to starboard, until she came to rest almost beam on to the sea. When this had occurred, her head would be toward the U-boat and her after gun could then no longer be made to bear on the enemy. Provided the German Kapitan appreciated the position, there would be a big arc ahead of the destroyer in which the enemy could maneuver with impunity, whilst he fired into the *Hecate's* unprotected bows until he had sunk her.

For the first time the Captain found his own confidence in the final outcome distinctly upset. The fates had been kind to the U-boat. The lucky chance of surfacing up-sun, the three hits, each in its own way tipping the scales more heavily against him—these had put him in an almost untenable position from which he could only be extricated if the wheel of fortune should turn once more.

Thank God the after gun was still firing! A white column of water rose ahead of the U-boat. Again the gun barked defiance. Wondering how much longer the gun would bear, and unable to see it because of the steam cloud, he turned to watch the fall of its shot. The U-boat now appeared to be beam on to the line of fire. Already it was moving slowly toward the arc of complete safety. For a moment it subsided into the hollow of a swell until only the conning tower and gun were visible. It rose swiftly as the sea passed under it. He could see the puff of yellowy-white smoke as its gun fired.

Then, miraculously, another more orange explosion occurred beneath the enemy muzzle, and a dark yellow blob of smoke hovered for an instant around the place where the orange flash had been. When the smoke cleared away, the gun barrel pointed aimlessly into the sky, and of the men who had tended it a moment before—there was no sign.

BOOK FOUR

Cold Steel

Thursday, 09.16
to Thursday, 11.32

WHEN von Stolberg again trained the periscope on to the destroyer, he saw the havoc that the last shot had caused to his enemy. It did not seem likely that she would steam again before he could complete her destruction. If only he could get ahead of her, so that her after gun would not be able to train on him, he could sink her at his leisure.

"Port twenty," he ordered.

Schwachofer repeated the order.

Slowly, desperately, the U-boat turned. Now there was hardly enough of a charge left in her one battery to keep her moving. Just as slowly the Kapitan moved around, grasping the periscope handles to keep the destroyer in view.

"Schwachofer, I believe she has stopped! Ask Braun if he can hear any propeller noise on the hydrophone. Her relative bearing now is approximately red nine-oh." The Kapitan was not again going to let the destroyer out of his sight.

"No, Herr Kapitan, she is stopped," the Oberleutnant reported back.

"It is very good. Soon we shall be out of the arc of fire of that after gun, and then we can sink the swine."

"There is very little left in the battery, Herr Kapitan."

"We only need a very little, Herr Oberleutnant. Once his gun cannot reach us, we shall stop the motor. In three hundred meters we shall be safe. Less than that, because as he stops he will lie beam on to the wind, and his head will come round toward us."

Schwachofer could sense the appalling suspense under which his Kapitan was laboring. The knuckles of the hands that grasped the periscope showed white— as white as ivory. The man was breathing heavily with excitement, and his tongue licked his dry lips.

Their own gun fired again.

A second later there was a shuddering crash. The sound of the explosion was interlaced with high-pitched screams. The noise died away and left a silence that was full of foreboding.

"Himmel!" von Stolberg cried, leaping to the forward door of the control room. The gloom of the forepart of the boat was shot with a beam of daylight that came from the open fore hatch. Down the hatch there now spiraled a wisp of brown smoke. To the Kapitan it looked as if a serpent was slithering into the boat. He stopped short as he saw Müller run up the ladder. The feet paused when the head and shoulders were in the air. Then the sea boots began to come down the ladder slowly.

"Well, Müller?" the Kapitan asked.

"Kaput, Herr Kapitan, kaput."

"The gun?"

"As I said, Herr Kapitan, kaput."

"And the gun crew?"

Müller met the Kapitan's stare with a glance that was strangely sullen. "They also." He paused and added, "Herr Kapitan." Then he turned and disappeared forward into the gloom.

The Kapitan made a mental note that either Müller's nerve was cracking or the man, left to himself, would have already surrendered. Whatever the cause, it was a matter that would need investigation. For himself, he saw no reason to doubt their ability, even without the gun, to hold out until the arrival of the *Cecilie*. Perhaps if he coddled the crew with logical explanations, or took them into his confidence more than he was able by his nature to do, there would have been less peculiar behavior developing among them.

The Kapitan hurried back to the periscope. "Midships—steady," he called as he placed his forehead once more against the rubber pad. "Good. I can no longer see the gun. Herr Oberleutnant, stop the motors."

"I do not think, Herr Kapitan, that the propellers will turn again, unless we can get the diesels going. The battery is quite flat."

Von Stolberg shrugged. "What matter? It's now nine o'clock, and we have but three hours to wait. Let us go with the engineer to see if it is possible to get a diesel running. But first I will order Kunz and Müller to reload at least one torpedo. You have sufficient air, Herr Oberleutnant, to fire?"

Schwachofer bent to inspect the dials of the air bottles. In the dim light filtering from the open hatch, they were difficult to read.

"I think enough to fire one torpedo. Possibly two. No more, Herr Kapitan."

"One is enough."

"It will not be easy to reload with the boat rolling like this."

"It is never easy, Herr Oberleutnant, to do one's duty. But we will reload at least one tube."

"Jawohl, Herr Kapitan."

The Kapitan led the way forward.

"Leutnant Kunz, Petty Officer Müller," von Stolberg called as he neared the foot of the forward ladder.

The two men appeared out of the gloom that shrouded the forward compartment.

"Reload one torpedo," the Kapitan ordered.

"It is very dark—almost too dark to see, Herr Kapitan," Kunz dared to remark.

"Herr Leutnant, you will carry out my order—and at once."

"Herr Kapitan," the petty officer spoke quietly. It might be supposed that his age and years of experience would entitle him to a hearing.

"What is it, Müller?"

"The boat rolls too much. We will damage the torpedo and possibly crush a man."

"Then load another torpedo."

The two men looked at each other. Schwachofer watched the battle, and his sympathy ran out to the petty officer—if only because his Kapitan had in his reply considered only the torpedo. Long years of training might inculcate obedience, but they could not of themselves create willingness. The petty officer's eyes fell from the Kapitan's face.

"At once, Petty Officer Müller. And report to me as soon as you have reloaded."

The Kapitan turned and, followed by Schwachofer and Kritz the engineer, stumped up the ladder.

To reload the heavy greasy torpedoes it was usual either to dive to a depth where there was no interference from the surface waves or else, if the sea were slight, to steam slowly with the boat's head into the waves. To manhandle the two-ton monsters, even with the aid of grabs and chain blocks, while there was any movement on the boat, could only be attempted with serious risk both to the torpedoes and the men. It would have been dangerous enough with the usual good lighting; in semidarkness it would be doubly so.

Von Stolberg blinked in the strong sunlight and was suddenly aware of his own tiredness. The party of three men stood for a moment looking at the wreck of the gun. The British shell had exploded underneath its mounting, flinging the muzzle up and back, snapping one of the trunnion brackets, and breaking the cradle. Nothing that they could conceivably do to it would ever enable another shot to be fired.

They passed on around the conning tower and paused to inspect its battered after end, and the wreck of the A.A. gun. There were two more places on the after casing where shells had hit; and the jagged ends of torn metal twisted upward, revealing the red lead with which the underside of the deck had been painted.

The yellow-green fumes still eddied in waves from the open after hatch that led directly to the engine room; and even to look down from the upwind side they had to hold their breath. From inside came a continuous stuttering sound as the great batteries below the engine-room floor consumed themselves. The fire was as much electrical as it was organic—for no flames could be created without oxygen.

"I wonder if we could get down in gas masks," Schwachofer suggested.

"I very much doubt it," the engineer replied. "There is no oxygen down there at all."

"We could perhaps use the oxygen escape masks?" von Stolberg asked.

"Herr Kapitan, no man could endure the heat. The floor plates will be too hot to stand on."

"Pour some water down and see," von Stolberg insisted.

The engineer hurried away to the fore hatch to call for a bucket to be passed up.

The Kapitan and his Executive Officer were left alone. There was a sharp metallic ping from close at hand. They looked at each other. "What the devil was that?" von Stolberg asked.

Both men turned to look at the destroyer. Half a mile away, she lay rolling in the swell. The cloud of steam and smoke was lighter now, but she still remained immovable, and with her bow toward them. A whine in the air above their heads convinced both the Germans. They jumped as one man into the shell-torn hole in the casing.

"One would have thought that we had given the British enough to do without their firing rifles at us," von Stolberg grumbled.

The engineer was coming back now around the side of the conning tower carrying a bucket.

"Be careful, Otto," Schwachofer called; "they are firing with rifles."

The U-boat's stern was pointing toward the destroyer, but one side of the casing offered a little protection. Kritz and his bucket disappeared over the side of the casing. Walking on the U-boat's hull, he crept along toward the other two. The waves, lapping the circular hull, soaked his legs and he swore roundly.

"Bring some water with you," von Stolberg ordered.

"There's so much in my boots that I needn't have gone for a bucket," the engineer complained when he reached them.

In a moment he had handed up a bucket of water and joined the others in their shelter. A bullet whined over them as he crouched down. It made a metallic ping as it crumpled against the conning tower.

"Zum Teufel—the swine shoots well," von Stolberg remarked.

"And he's watching us the whole time," Schwachofer answered.

"It is impossible to get to the engine-room hatch on the protected side because of the fumes," Kritz informed them. "But there is shelter for one in the casing beside the hatch. If, Herr Kapitan, you will trust my report, I will go and pour some water down."

"Herr Kapitan, I submit," Schwachofer spoke, "that I should do so. You have only one engineer and if he were to be wounded or killed——" He did not finish the sentence.

"You are right, Herr Oberleutnant. Kritz, let Schwachofer have the bucket."

Gathering himself, the Executive Officer made a dash for the after hatch. It was only ten feet away, and he arrived comfortably before the enemy had seen him and had the chance to send a bullet after him. A second sufficed to pour the water down the open hatch and to hear the sizzle of steam as it splashed on the deck below. In a minute, jettisoning the bucket, Schwachofer had rejoined his companions.

"Well?" the Kapitan asked.

"It is, as the engineer says, quite hopeless. The plates are so hot that the water turned at once to steam."

"Then let us go back and torpedo the swine."

One by one they leapt over the edge of the casing and made their way forward. Once past the conning tower they were hidden from the marksmen on the destroyer and could climb back on to the casing's top.

From below, as they descended the ladder, came a heavy rumbling noise, shouts of alarm mingled with cries of pain, and then the sound of voices raised in anger.

The Kapitan stormed into the dark space of the forward torpedo room.

"Silence," he barked. "Stand back, all of you."

Following his commanding officer, Schwachofer could dimly discern the shining bulk of a torpedo lying diagonally across the confined space. Above it the two grabs swung silently from their chains. The Kapitan's call for silence had been obeyed by everyone except the man who lay prone beneath that great silvery tube. Falling from its grabs, the two-ton masterpiece of machinery had pinned one of the handlers to the deck. His agonized whimperings filled the dimly lit cavern—a terrible strain to nerves that were already stretched to breaking point.

The Kapitan bent to look at the fallen monster.

"Both rudders and the propeller damaged. Herr Leutnant Kunz, how did this happen?"

"Petty Officer Müller had omitted to see that the after grab was properly secured."

"That is a lie, Herr Kapitan."

"Petty Officer, wait until you are spoken to."

"It is a lie," the man repeated.

"Be quiet, Müller," the Kapitan ordered with fury.

"I cannot be quiet, Herr Kapitan, when this young fool accuses me of something I have never done," Müller answered with considerable dignity.

The probability that he was being forced to back the wrong horse only made the Kapitan more angry. Discipline had to be maintained. The words spoken by a knowledgeable petty officer about an inexperienced young officer may have been right, but leaving the position as it was would have done incalculable damage. In any case the words seemed to von Stolberg to strike at the very root of the discipline that he maintained—a discipline that in its Germanic strictness set the officers as unquestionably superior to the men just because they were officers, and not because they had proved worthy of obedience. The situation, common enough in the fighting service of any nation, struck at the weakest link in the German armor—and left the Kapitan groping for a correct solution that his own nature and training denied him. As each second ticked by, he became more and more aware that his decision, when it came, would lose him the services of one of the most experienced men in his crew.

"Herr Oberleutnant," he addressed Schwachofer, and his voice sounded unutterably weary. "Petty Officer Müller is to be placed under open arrest for insulting an officer."

"Jawohl, Herr Kapitan." As Schwachofer came forward, he thought that the day continued to grow more and more awful. Had they not, he wondered, sufficient with which to contend without falling into this kind of conflict among themselves?

"Petty Officer Müller," Schwachofer called, and turned to lead the way back to the control room. Dazedly Müller stumbled after him. It now seemed unthinkable that he had ever dared to defy authority —however unreasonable it had been.

"Now," von Stolberg said, "we will lift the fore end of the torpedo and release Schott. Then we'll chock this torpedo on the deck here, and bring out another. And I will take charge of the loading."

THE DAMAGE to the destroyer was even worse than was at first supposed.

The shell, in entering the ship's side, had severed the steering rods that connected the wheel in the bridge superstructure with the steering engine that was right aft and above the rudder head. Even if her crew should get her steaming again, the helm orders would have to be passed by telephone from the bridge to the auxiliary hand-steering in the tiller flat.

The shell, exploding on the side of number two boiler, had been directly beneath the platform of the starboard Oerlikon gun. The force of the explosion had lifted the stalk clear of the deck and flung the gun from its bedplate.

The damage in the boiler rooms could not be assessed until the fire had been put out in the first and the steam had been allowed to clear from the second. When at last an inspection was made, it was found that number one boiler could never be used because of the fractured steampipe; number two had been wrecked beyond repair by the shell; and only from number three could there be any hope of obtaining steam. But even to that boiler considerable damage had been done, not primarily by the shell itself but by the distortion of the boiler tubes during rapid cooling after the steam had left the boiler.

The engineer officer, going to the bridge to make his report, found the Captain, rifle in hand, taking careful aim at the small target that lolloped lazily over the swell ahead of them.

"Just keeping the enemy awake," the Captain explained. "Well, Chief, what's your report?"

"I can probably get some sort of steam on number three in about an hour, sir. But it won't be much—enough to move the ship. I can't promise more than that, sir."

"You can't do better than your best, anyway. Let me know when I can move her—then I'm going to ram the ruddy U-boat. That is, if it stays where it is. I've been looking at it through the binoculars. It seems to have a pretty good fire going in its after end —probably the batteries. One or two of their chaps have been trying to look down the after hatch—the one that all the smoke is coming from. But they don't seem able to get below, so I assume that they can't motor off."

The First Lieutenant joined them. He saluted the Captain. "Permission to take away the motorboat and whaler with a boarding party, sir?"

The Captain thought for a moment. "Right, Chief," he dismissed the engineer. "Ring the telegraphs when you're ready." Then, turning to his Executive Officer: "No, I don't think so, Number One. There are at least forty very angry Herrenfolk in that tin cigar. They'd pick you off as easy as wink. If we could give you any real supporting fire from the ship, it would be a different matter. Then you could lay off and lob hand grenades down the fore hatch. But as things are, I don't fancy it. With rifles at this range, we'd be as likely to hit the boats as the Ube. But I'll tell you what you can do—if you feel that doing something is better than doing nothing—you can put the boats in the water and try to tow our stern around a bit so that the after gun can get a shot or two away. You've probably more chance of towing the stern upwind. Even if you can stop the stern from moving, maybe the bow will blow down and give us the twist we need. Better forget about the bow oar in the whaler and put two men on each of the other four. If the Chief can give us steam, I'll not hoist in the boats before I ram the U-boat. They'll be available then, either for picking up survivors or for a boarding party. So take some ammunition in the motorboat, a couple of rifles and revolvers, and good luck to you."

When the First Lieutenant's feet had clattered down the ladder, the Captain had nothing immediately to claim his attention. Never since he had joined the *Hecate* five months before had there ever been such a deathly hush on the bridge. For with the loss of her steam the big dynamos had died; and without them there was no electricity, and hence nothing of those instruments that depended on that power. There was no asdic, no radar, and no wireless. Small effects like the clicking of the pitometer log

167

were missed; and the little lights, used to denote that their part of the ship was ready to function correctly, no longer burned. The masterpieces of machinery, and the intricacies of the instruments, were dead and useless when the essential steam that fed them was no longer available.

The Yeoman came to him. "Johnson has found the signal to Force M, sir." He handed the Captain the message board.

"Force M from Admiralty.

"Detach Acheron, Marabout, Mastiff to join Hecate shadowing U-boat at 0800 in position 06° 35′ N. 30° 10′ W. Course 210° four knots. Anticipate U-boat may be attempting to rendezvous with Raider S or Raider M. Important to reduce wireless traffic to absolute minimum."

The Captain handed the pad back and said with a smile: "Such a minimum of traffic that they did not repeat the signal to us. I suppose this was just in case we should start chattering to *Acheron* to tell her what we were doing, and where we were doing it. For all that, I think we'd better call her up now on the emergency transmitter and tell her exactly where we are. Make to *Acheron: 'Have brought U-boat to surface. Am repairing shell damage preparatory to ramming. My position 5° N. 32° W.'* Be sure it's coded."

"Aye aye, sir." Willis took the pad and hurried from the bridge.

The Captain's spirits had been raised by the chance appearance of the Yeoman, for in that very ordinary transaction he saw a return to the normal conditions on the bridge.

The next visitor was Robins.

"I'm sorry we're a little late today, sir," he said to the astonished Captain, as he spread a clean white napkin on the chart table and began to unpack the breakfast plates and to set the knives and fork tidily beside them. " 'Fraid it's reconstituted again, sir."

"Frankly, Robins, I think you're a marvel. I hadn't expected anything until this business was over."

"You never know when it will be over, do you, sir? Not with these Huns. Very determined people, Germans—ambitious too."

The Captain saw that his steward was looking ahead through the glass of the windshield.

"Is that her, sir?"

"That's the cause of all the trouble. Take my glasses if you'd like a better look."

While Robins focused the glasses on the enemy from which the smoke still rose in lazy rolls, the Captain ate hurriedly. By the time he had finished the scrambled eggs, the Yeoman was back again. "Message passed, sir," he reported.

"Did she sound near?" the Captain asked.

"Can't say, sir. But the range of the emergency set isn't all that great, and she 'came up' at once and as soon as we called her."

A telegraphist had come on the bridge with a signal that he gave to the Yeoman, who handed it to the Captain.

The message read: *"Acheron to Hecate. Expect to arrive your position 1200 today."*

"That's heartening to know anyway," the Captain said as he handed it back.

Both the boats were now in the water and were trying to haul the destroyer's stern round. But the scend of the sea was proving too much for them to overcome; and it was soon only too obvious that they could accomplish nothing.

Going to the loud-hailer to tell them to lay off, the Captain realized that that was just one more piece of equipment that would no longer work. As he had little hope of reaching the boats with a megaphone from the bridge, he went aft himself.

Leaning over the guard rails, he shouted to the First Lieutenant. Having attracted his attention, he told him to bring the boats to lie under the ship's lee.

"It's no good, Number One. You haven't moved her more than a degree or two, and to be any use you'd have to shift her through at least twenty-five degrees. You'd better wait until I've found out from the Chief when he thinks he'll have steam." With that he hurried down to the boiler room.

There the engineer was just flashing up a torch for the third boiler.

"Well, Chief?"

"Not too good, sir. Take a peep through the inspection port. You can see the tubes hanging in bights. But with luck we'll be able to give you some sort of steam."

"I don't want much. Just enough to ram the boat. Even three or four knots would be sufficient if we went at her down sea. We'd just push her under."

"With the tubes like that, I've got to take it gently. About twenty minutes, I reckon."

"That'll have to do."

The Captain climbed the long ladders back to the deck.

"Chief's just flashing up now," he shouted to the

First Lieutenant. "He thinks that he can give us steam in twenty minutes." He glanced at his watch. "That means about half-past ten. I think the boats had better take a box of grenades each, and lay about half a mile off the U-boat. Send the motorboat upwind to the westward, and you take the whaler half a mile downwind of her. If she tries to move, the chances are that she won't be able to go very fast, and you might be able to intercept her. Don't start anything unless you have to—much better to let me ram her."

On his way back to the bridge he went forward into the sick bay. Ellis had been joined by the burned stokers from the forward boiler room. They were injected to the limit with morphine and lay swathed in bandages, sleeping the merciful sleep that science had given them.

"Well, Doctor?"

"Not so bad, sir. They're terribly burned, and I'd like to get them into a proper hospital as soon as we can. But they'll be all right for the moment. When can we steam, sir?"

The question was not to be wondered at. There is no sensation more trying to a seaman than to be in a steel vessel whose engines have ceased to turn. In the moment that the metallic heartbeats die away, it is as if some part of one's own body has ceased to function. Until the propellers stopped, it had seemed inevitable that this metal creature should reach its journey's end. With their stopping, doubts were raised. Small at first, the fears mounted as silent hour followed silent hour. In time the strain would endanger reason more surely and more subtly than the worst of storms. A sailor's trade, be he master or crew, is to move

171

ships from one part of the world to another. Failure to do this will strike at the root of his being.

"Very soon now, Doc. I'm going to ram as soon as the Chief has got steam on his kettle. If you'd like to come up and watch the fun, do so."

"Thanks. I will. As soon as I feel her move. I can't do anything more for these chaps."

The Captain went back to the bridge. It had not seemed twenty minutes since he'd been in the boiler room. He had hardly arrived when the Coxswain was calling up the voice pipe. "Engine room's rung the telegraphs, sir."

"Thank you, Coxswain." He was panting after his climb. Suddenly he realized that he had been without sleep since eight o'clock on Tuesday morning, and it was now almost Thursday noon. Fifty hours. Strangely, he felt less tired than he had the previous day. "Coxswain, you'd better get down to the after-steering position. It is connected up. I'll have to conn you by telephone. If you find her heavy on the wheel, you can get plenty of men from the depth-charge crews. Report on the telephone as soon as you're ready."

3

VON STOLBERG and Schwachofer, driving their men like furies, had succeeded in reloading two bow tubes; but unless they could turn the boat around, they could still not fire them at the destroyer. With perspiration running down their faces they had gone back to the control room.

"Kritz," von Stolberg spoke to the engineer, "I want to see if there is anything left in the battery. The boat will turn more easily downwind. Use only the starboard engine." And to the quartermaster, Schrader: "Put your rudder hard over to port."

"Hard-a-port," Schrader repeated.

The Kapitan nodded at the engineer.

The switches were made. For a second that was agony to the men who had worked so hard, no sound came. Then very slowly a gentle purring noise was heard.

"Starboard motor turning," Kritz's voice came in

a whisper. The four Germans looked at each other and breathed deeply.

The motion of the boat changed. The seas were astern of her. She hung poised on one and then her stern slid gracefully into the hollow. When it rose again the force of the next sea swung her around rapidly.

"Stop the motor," von Stolberg ordered, and trained the periscope.

"Stand by tubes." He gave the order to Schwachofer, and then for a moment took his eyes from the lenses and looked at his officers.

"Gentlemen. We will sink him now. Ja. It is good. You are ready, Herr Oberleutnant?"

"Numbers one and two tubes are ready, Herr Kapitan."

"Start the motor again; she will come around slowly. Ah—very soon now—very soon. Stand by, my dear Schwachofer—and stand by, you damn British ——" A longer pause. "Du lieber Gott, he is moving! Kritz! Give her every bit of power you have."

"There is no more, Herr Kapitan."

"Port, you fool—hard-a-port."

"The rudder is hard over, Herr Kapitan."

"The motor has stopped, Herr Kapitan."

Von Stolberg raised his head and shoulders from the periscope. Schwachofer was astonished that any face could change so much in so short a time.

"Can we not angle the torpedoes?" Kritz suggested.

"What? Without electricity to set the attack table?" von Stolberg sneered.

The three Germans looked at each other.

"The *Cecilie* will be here in one hour and twenty minutes," the Kapitan murmured.

"I fear the destroyer may be here first," Schwachofer said.

"He cannot sink us by gunfire." From Kritz.

"He will ram us—if he has any sense," the Kapitan said. On the ladder that led to the conning tower, he turned and added, "And I fear that he has. Unlock the revolver cabinet and take one each." While one hand grasped the ladder he extended the other toward the engineer.

As soon as the revolver had been handed to him, the Kapitan climbed up the ladder.

4

STARBOARD TWENTY," the Captain spoke into the telephone handset.

Slowly, very slowly, the destroyer began to move. Her head turned away from her enemy as she set out in a big quarter-circle. She would make her final approach on her opponent's beam, where the blow that she intended to deal would be sure to be lethal.

"Midships. Yeoman, signal to the boats to close in."

"Aye aye, sir."

"Port five. Pilot, tell the gunnery officer to open fire whenever he can."

"Aye aye, sir."

"Midships."

The after gun began to fire steadily. Shots once more fell about the U-boat, and two more hits were scored. Then the gun stopped as the *Hecate* began to turn toward her quarry.

"Gunnery officer reports that target is obscured, sir." The navigator had the phone.

"Tell Guns that it's cold steel now," the Captain answered.

Slowly and sedately the *Hecate* advanced. Coming downwind and sea, she moved gracefully, her high bow with its long knife-edge rising and falling as it cleft the seas in two.

"Port twenty." Sunlight flooded the scene. The blue-green waves were dancing; the graceful ship bowing to the swell; and so, too, the equally graceful, if serpentine, U-boat. Here was no battle fever—only the grim determination to wipe out an enemy craft, to avenge the damage done to herself and the death of her men. Was that all? The Captain wondered. No, it wasn't all.

He sensed rather than saw the Doctor beside him, and was glad of the company of his friend.

"Starboard twenty." At slow speed, downsea, and with the rudder in the hand-steering that was so much slower than her steering engine, it was proving very difficult to keep the *Hecate* on a steady course. The Captain could imagine the sweating men working feverishly at the big hand wheel. Had he realized just how difficult it would be to steer her down the seas, he would have turned the other way and come upwind against the enemy. It was too late to change; and although he did not know it, the U-boat would have torpedoed him had he turned to port.

Closing now. Very close. They could see the conning tower plainly and a flaxen-haired man standing there.

"Port twenty."

Suddenly the Captain was aware of a rifle raised beside him. One of the signalmen had seized the weapon and was about to aim at the solitary figure that stood on the conning tower.

The Captain leapt at the gun and seized it from the astonished sailor's hand. "What the hell do you think you're doing?—that's murder." Then realizing the apparent injustice of his act, when only a short while before he himself had been firing at the U-boat, he was forced to spend further time in explanation. "It's quite different now, Higgins. Before, there was a chance that they could get the boat under way and torpedo us. Now they haven't an earthly—and in a moment they will be survivors."

The seconds that had flown by were precious ones, and they could have been otherwise employed. A wave, just sufficiently irregular in comparison with its fellows, rose a little to port of the destroyer's stern. The destroyer was already carrying twenty degrees of port rudder, and the bow swung rapidly to port, passing the conning tower of the U-boat at which the Captain had been aiming.

"Hard-a-starboard."

Below the men sweated to obey the order, heaving around the heavy wheel that, with its low gearing, meant so many turns must be made before the rudder could be moved from one side to the other.

The *Hecate's* knife-edged bow was poised threateningly above the low hull of the U-boat as it lay in the trough. The wave that had slewed the destroyer's stern and in passing under her had raised her bow, now flung up the hull of *U-121* at the same moment that its forward motion allowed the *Hecate's* bow to slice down.

178

With a seering crash and a scream of tortured steel, the bow bit deeply into the metal flank. The strong hull of the submarine could not withstand the blow that the destroyer had dealt—even if it had not been truly aimed.

As the destroyer's bow cut through the ballast tanks and stove in the inch-thick pressure hull, the U-boat heeled. The German officer's arm shot up. For a moment before the man was tumbled into the sea, the Captain glimpsed a revolver aimed at himself. He was almost sorry that he had stopped the signalman from firing.

The *Hecate* had dealt her enemy a mortal wound; but it was a glancing blow, and it should have been a straight one. The U-boat was forced around by her assailant until the two ships lay side by side and beam on to the sea. The sharp port hydroplane at the U-boat's stern penetrated the plating of the destroyer's second, and largest, boiler room. Rolling apart as the waves' crest passed under them, the two vessels were flung together again in the succeeding trough. With her momentum the *Hecate* had moved forward; and this time the hydroplane, like a deadly fang, punctured the plating of the engine room.

The Captain, on the bridge, was aware of the disaster. It was only the extent of the damage that remained in doubt.

Followed by the Doctor, he had moved hurriedly to the after end of the bridge, where the long ladders rose in two flights from the main deck thirty feet below. Members of the boiler-room and engine-room crews were already standing between the funnels, and more and more of their mates joined them. Along the rails were many men of the ship's company, gathered

179

to help the survivors climb aboard. But they were nearly all leaning over to see the damage that was being done to their own ship; and the U-boat's men, who now poured out of her fore hatch and conning tower and who had expected help to climb aboard the ship that had destroyed their boat, found no help offered. They set about abandoning their vessel in their own yellow rubber dinghies, some of which were already pushing off from the far side.

From the bridge it was very difficult to find out what was happening below. The Captain was just about to slide down the ladder when he saw the urgent figure of the engineer pushing through the crowd. The Chief paused at the foot of the ladder and, looking up, saw the Captain above him.

"What chance, Chief?" the Captain called.

"Without full steam to work the ejectors, absolutely none, sir."

"How many compartments will flood?"

"Number two boiler room and the engine room."

"We'll not be able to keep her afloat."

"I don't reckon so, sir. The shell burst the bulkhead between number one and two boiler room, and that will flood too."

Dumfounded by the magnitude of the disaster that had overtaken his ship, the Captain beat his mind to think. The engine room was the biggest single compartment in the ship. With it and the two boiler-rooms flooded, half her buoyancy would be lost. In ramming the U-boat he had been prepared to lose the small amount of buoyancy represented by the fore-peak—and even with the flooding of the forward magazine occasioned by the fire, he had accepted the loss of the former without fear for his ship. But these flooded compartments, added to the loss of boiler and engine rooms, made the end certain.

"We'll abandon ship, Chief," he called down to the upturned face below him. Then, turning back to the front of the bridge: "Get your sick cases on deck, Doctor—port side. I'll get the motorboat alongside to take them off," and to the Yeoman: "Tell the motorboat to come alongside port side for the wounded."

"Aye aye, sir."

"Signalman. Take the official publications down to the wireless cabinet. Tell Johnson to make an SOS to *Acheron* on the emergency set and then abandon ship. Make sure the door of the cabinet is locked when the last man is out."

He saw the navigator beside him. "Pilot, have stations for abandoning ship piped, and then get down to the main deck and give a hand getting the lifesaving equipment over the side."

For the moment he was alone on the bridge with nothing more to do. He glanced over the side at the U-boat, which was now obviously sinking. His own ship felt heavier and less lively. She wallowed drunkenly in the swell instead of rising delicately over its ridges. The last of the U-boat's men were leaving her, and already his own men were starting to go over the side.

He was too tired to feel annoyance. Too tired even to feel any anger against the enemy. Slowly he went down to the main deck.

BOOK FIVE

Fisticuffs

Thursday, 11.32
to Thursday, 12.05

1

THE SEA was full of bobbing heads when both the destroyer and U-boat had sunk beneath the waves. In the center of the crowd the yellow rubber dinghies from the submarine and the gray Carley Floats from the destroyer rose and fell in the seas. The two crews were inextricably mixed, and there were as many Germans in the Carley Floats as there were British seamen in the dinghies. Once the ships had gone, they were no longer Germans and British sailors but common survivors of a similar ordeal. Men of either nation helped each other to clamber into a boat, or swam companionably alongside men whom they had been indirectly trying to slay a moment before.

The Captain swam to a Carley Float and, half climbing into it, was helped the rest of the way by a sailor who was already there.

"Hallo, sir," the man said, "didn't recognize you at first, sir."

185

"That's all right, Thomas—filthy stuff, this fuel oil, especially when it's mixed with the diesel from the U-boat."

There were four other men in the raft, three sailors from the destroyer and one German. Another hand appeared, grasping desperately alongside.

"Get him in," the Captain said. "He's got no life jacket."

The man was hauled into the boat. The two and a half gold stripes and the star on his cuffs told their own tale. The two Captains were in the same raft.

At the moment when the Captain recognized the still-panting German, he was himself identified. The newcomer struggled to his feet as the British Captain sat down.

"Korvettan Kapitan Peter von Stolberg," the Kapitan announced. The raft rolled as it passed over the top of the swell, and von Stolberg nearly went over the side.

"It is surprising how big the sea is when you take to it in a raft," the Captain said.

"That is so. You are the Captain?"

"Yes, I am the Captain."

The Kapitan made sure of his balance and placed his legs far apart.

"We have sunk ourselves," he announced.

"More correctly, I sank you, and then was fool enough to let my ship be driven into yours."

The German shrugged.

"Won't you sit down?"

"I do not yet know your name, Herr Captain."

The Captain tried again. "Do sit down."

"I prefer to stand."

"You've kept me awake for the last two nights. Excuse me if I do not join you."

Finally, despite himself, von Stolberg sat down on the opposite side of the raft. As it rocked over the waves, the two Captains adjusted their balance, first one—then the other. They had the ludicrous appearance of a couple of mandarins bowing to each other alternately.

"We must discuss business," the Kapitan said.

"Business? Perhaps so, but may I ask you some questions? What I really want to know is where you went yesterday morning. Did you double back and then make a big circle to the southeast before you returned to your course of two-one-oh?"

"Herr Captain"—the German drew himself up stiffly—"you know my course?"

"I've come a long enough way with you! Over two hundred miles. Where exactly were you going?"

"I do not think, Herr Captain, that I can answer your questions. The circumstances, you will agree, are very peculiar."

"I should say that they were unique. But I don't see why we can't discuss what we've been trying to do to each other for the past forty hours."

"I prefer not to talk about the duties of my ship."

"Well, I suppose that is the absolutely correct attitude to adopt. Though it does seem a pity. When we hauled you aboard, I'd hoped we might have enjoyed a sort of nineteenth hole."

Von Stolberg raised his eyebrows. "I do not understand."

"Don't you play golf? I thought you Continentals played a lot."

The Captain took fresh stock of his ex-enemy, whom he now felt that he should treat as a guest. However he had to admit that, as host, he had so far been unable to make a breech in the German's reserve. Von Stolberg was obviously recovering from the exertion of his swim, and the Captain could only hope that, when he had fully recovered, he would prove a more congenial companion.

"Herr Captain," von Stolberg began again. "We have business to discuss."

"Oh, not really! All I expect from you is that you will keep discipline among your men, and I'll look after mine. Not that any of them look as if they're going to cause trouble." The Captain glanced round at the mixed nationalities that bobbed and floated all around. "But I do wish you'd tell me where you were going. I promised my Doctor that I'd ask you that."

"Herr Captain. I have arrived."

"Congratulations! You know, I said to my navigator only this morning, when we got our morning stars, that I thought you might have done so. Of course I forgot—you couldn't take any yourself. However, you might like to know that your dead reckoning was exactly right——"

The German, speaking sharply, interrupted him. "Herr Captain. Your ship's name, if you please?"

"My ship is—was—His Majesty's Destroyer *Hecate*. And the number of your U-boat?" the Captain asked, supposing that he must overlook the peremptory tone of the German's question.

"Herr Captain, I am not at liberty to disclose the number of my U-boat."

The Englishman was genuinely puzzled by this apparently discourteous and unreasonable reply. He tried again. "You know, von Stolberg, you are adopting a peculiar attitude. I've told you the name of my ship, and I don't see why you can't tell me the number of yours."

"Herr Captain. I think you overlook something."

"I don't see what. We're both survivors. Surely we can be civil to each other?"

The German rose solemnly to his feet. The raft gave a vicious lurch and von Stolberg again nearly went overboard. Recovering himself and placing his legs well apart, he began to speak.

"Herr Captain, I must make myself plain. You are my prisoner."

"I am your *what?*" The Captain was shocked into sitting bolt upright.

"You are my prisoner. The German Armed Cruiser *Cecilie* meets me here at noon today. Already she has many Allied prisoners. You and your men will join them."

The Captain flogged his tired brain to think. He was longing to tell this piece of Junkerdom that if the *Cecilie* had been invited to a party in 5 North, 32 Degrees West, he also had asked three guests of his own to attend. As he fought back the temptation to do so, he noticed that the German looked at his watch. "I hope yours has stopped—mine has," he said with venom.

The German was not amused. "I ask you to give me your parole."

"Look, if you want a fight, you can have one. If I were to tell my lads to wade in and chuck the whole lot of your forty-odd men into the ditch—they'd do it. I don't want that to happen, but if I have one more word about my being your prisoner—I'll slap your ears back myself. Now sit down before I knock you down."

Sustained by duty, succoured by confidence in the early arrival of the *Cecilie,* and quite unable to envisage the resumption of any form of warfare, von Stolberg, his speech slowed by incredulity, answered: "But, Herr Captain, you are going to be my———"

"I'm going to be your—what?"

"My prisoner."

"Come and get me then." The Captain had not felt so physically angry since he had left school. He rose to his feet.

Leading Seaman Thomas rose with him.

"No—no, Thomas. He's my bird. I'm going to dust his pants for him." The Captain put his hand on the sailor's shoulder and forced him to sit again.

"You would not strike me? You, an officer, to fight like a peasant?"

"I'm a survivor and you're another—one that I particularly do not like."

"Sock 'im hard, sir. Don't waste time on the bastard." Thomas sounded gleeful.

The Captain did so. The German stumbled on the rocking raft and came back madly like a bull.

Whether or not the British sailors would have left the two to fight it out alone, no one will ever know; because in the next raft Kunz seized a paddle and flung it heavily across the intervening stretch of water. It caught the British Captain between the shoulder-blades.

At the same moment as Kunz threw it, Stoker

Bradley who sat next to him, and who only a moment before had offered the German a cigarette, whipped out his monkey wrench and smashed in the young Nazi's head.

What the moment before had been a party of ship-wrecked sailors bobbing companionably over the swell was now a waving sea of arms and legs as the occupants of each frail craft locked in deadly combat.

The rumpus had gone on for ten minutes when it was brought to a sudden panting hush. The Hecates, whose numbers were gradually prevailing in each raft, raised their eyes to the source of the sound.

"And what the hell is going on here?" the unmistakably English voice had asked. Then again from the destroyer's bridge the loud-hailer blared as, with engines churning in reverse, she lay stopped in the swell. "HMS *Marabout,* at your service. Now look lively there, and get aboard as quickly as you can. *Acheron* and *Mastiff* are sinking a German raider just over the horizon. We want to see the fun too."